Cat felt a hard jolt back of her SUV...

The back window exploded, cold night air whistling through the opening. Her SUV began to fishtail. She hung on to the wheel, fighting to right the vehicle without going off the shoulderless road. She'd only just gained control when she looked in her rearview mirror.

The truck seemed to back off. What was the driver doing? Then she saw it. He was going to make another run at her, to increase his speed. This time he planned to hit her harder in an attempt to drive her off the road.

Dylan could feel his pickup's tires digging into the dirt as he roared back behind Cat and the truck. He hadn't known this kind of fear in a very long time. He'd never had this much on the line. This was personal. He felt responsible for Cat and her baby. He had to stop the truck after them—no matter what he had to do...

MISSING: BABY DOE

B.J. DANIELS

Harlequin

INTRIGUE

This book is dedicated to my granddaughter Alayna, who always has a notebook and pen with her. May she write her own books one day.

Harlequin®
INTRIGUE™

Recycling programs for this product may not exist in your area.

ISBN-13: 978-1-335-45720-2

Missing: Baby Doe

Copyright © 2025 by Barbara Heinlein

 Harlequin Enterprises ULC
22 Adelaide St. West, 41st Floor
Toronto, Ontario M5H 4E3, Canada
www.Harlequin.com

Printed in Lithuania

MIX
Paper | Supporting responsible forestry
FSC® C021394

New York Times and *USA TODAY* bestselling author **B.J. Daniels** lives in Montana with her husband, Parker, and three springer spaniels. When not writing, she quilts, boats and plays tennis. Contact her at bjdaniels.com, on Facebook or on X, @bjdanielsauthor.

Books by B.J. Daniels

Harlequin Intrigue

Renegade Wife

Silver Stars of Montana

Big Sky Deception
Missing: Baby Doe

A Colt Brothers Investigation

Murder Gone Cold
Sticking to Her Guns
Christmas Ransom
Set Up in the City
Her Brand of Justice
Dead Man's Hand

Canary Street Press

Powder River

Dark Side of the River
River Strong
River Justice

Visit the Author Profile page at Harlequin.com.

CAST OF CHARACTERS

Acting Sheriff Catherine "Cat" Jameson—The widow had her own reasons for taking the temporary job in Fortune Creek.

Lindsey Martin—Very pregnant, the woman claimed to be running for her life—and that of her baby's.

Dylan Walker—The recluse widower rancher claimed he'd never impregnated anyone and didn't know the alleged woman.

Helen Graves—The elderly sheriff's department dispatcher knew more than anyone suspected.

Rowena Keeling—She claimed to have been the perfect friend to Dylan's deceased wife.

Ginny Cooper Walker—The deceased wife had more than a few secrets of her own.

Athena Grant—She found herself in a dangerous group with one special thing in common.

Chapter One

The front door of the Fortune Creek, Montana, Sheriff's Department swung open with a swoosh. A gust of cold mountain air blew in along with a frantic and very pregnant brunette.

Acting Sheriff Catherine "Cat" Jameson looked up in surprise. Since she'd taken over the job here while the sheriff was on his honeymoon, she'd come to believe that nothing happened in this tiny town in the northwest corner of the state. Certainly nothing that required a sheriff—or even an acting one.

"You have to help me!" the woman cried.

Cat's first thought was that the woman was in labor and about to have her baby right here in this office. Her own hand went to her much smaller baby bump. By the time she gave birth a couple of months from now, her job here as acting sheriff would be over. That was as far into the future as she let herself plan.

As the pregnant woman rushed toward the acting sheriff's minuscule office, Cat wished she'd done more reading on the delivery part of pregnancy. Dispatcher Helen Graves, a gray-haired sixty-something tank of a woman, could and would stop a freight train from getting past her and into Sheriff Brandt Parker's office. But as the brunette lumbered past, Helen simply shrugged.

So that's how it's going to be, Cat thought, getting to her feet. Apparently, the dispatcher-receptionist was only protective of *Sheriff* Parker, who had recently *extended* his honeymoon.

"Please," the brunette cried, cupping her protruding baby bump protectively.

Cat's mind whirled. The nearest hospital was miles away. Calling an ambulance would only waste time. Helen, she doubted, would be of any help. Cat would have to take the woman to Eureka in her patrol SUV and hope they got there in time.

It was the next words out of the pregnant woman's mouth that sidelined those thoughts. "He's going to kill me and my baby."

"Wait." Cat thought she'd heard wrong. "You aren't in labor?" Head shake. "You believe someone is trying to kill you and your baby?" Hurried nod. Delivering a baby was out of Cat's wheelhouse, but attempted murder? She told herself that the woman had come to the right place. This is what she'd been trained for. Also, she definitely needed a case she could sink her teeth into before she died of boredom at this isolated outpost only a stone's throw from the Canadian border.

Then again, wasn't that why she'd gotten the job? Because she was pregnant, no one would hire her except for a desk position. Fortune Creek was the definition of a sleepy wilderness.

"No one is going to kill you or the baby in here," Cat assured her. "Please have a seat," she said as she reached for her box of tissues.

As the brunette awkwardly lowered herself into a chair, Cat slid the box across the desk to her. "Why don't we start with your name?"

"Lindsey," the woman said and blew her nose into a tissue. "Lindsey Martin."

As she watched Lindsey pull herself together, Cat took the measure of the woman. Late twenties, early thirties, about her own age. Manicured and polished from her nails to her hair. No apparent shortage of funds, given the SUV parked out front and her clothing and footwear—not to mention her watch and other jewelry.

Lindsey Martin still looked terrified, glancing over her shoulder toward the empty street every few moments, but she'd quit crying.

"Lindsey, can you tell me why you think you and your baby are at risk?"

"It's the father of my baby." A domestic situation. So far Cat had only had to break up a bar fight while in charge in Fortune Creek. "He's denying that it's even his baby."

"I see. How long have the two of you been together?"

The woman looked confused. "We aren't together."

"Okay, maybe you need to start at the beginning."

Lindsey took a few breaths. She was pretty, her long hair tucked up in a twist on the left side of her head with an obvious expertise that Cat had never mastered. The woman's eyes were a rich chocolate brown, her olive skin well-tended. She either didn't wear makeup or her tears had washed it away. "I met him nine months ago in Washington, DC."

"Love at first sight?"

"*Hardly.* It was supposed to be a one-night stand.

We'd both been drinking. He said he had protection. I think he put something in my drink because I don't remember anything after that until I woke up…pregnant." She glanced down at her extended belly.

This was definitely not the romantic story gone wrong that Cat had been expecting. "Are you saying you were assaulted?"

She hesitated. "It was consensual—but…" She glanced down at her extended abdomen. "This wasn't part of the deal."

Cat sat back. "I'm confused. If you thought you'd been drugged, did you go to the police and report it?" She already knew the answer even before the woman shook her head. Otherwise, Lindsey Martin wouldn't be here now. "What brought you to Fortune Creek?"

"My baby's father bought a ranch and moved out here. When I couldn't reach him by phone, I drove out here to confront him."

"From Washington, DC?" Cat asked in surprise.

"No, I've been living in Denver. He wouldn't even talk to me, let alone allow me on his property."

"You said he threatened to harm you and the baby?"

"I left him a note in his mailbox with my phone number and where I was staying in Eureka. This morning, I got this." She reached into her shoulder bag, dug around and came up with a sheet of folded paper. Slapping it down on Cat's desk, she said, "It was pushed under my motel room door at the address I'd left him."

Cat drew out latex gloves before picking up the sheet of paper and unfolding it. *Stop causing trouble or I'll get rid of both you and your baby permanently.* It wasn't signed. She looked from the words to Lindsey and back. "You're sure this is from the father of the baby?"

"Who else?"

Exactly. "And you say this is the first time you've contacted him?" A nod. "Is there anyone else who might wish you harm?"

"In Montana?" She let out a laugh that was close to a sob. "Even if there was, he's the only person who even knows I'm in Montana."

"Okay. Do you mind if I keep this?" Lindsey shook her head. Cat bagged the note and asked, "You're sure you've never tried contacting him before this? Because the note makes it sound like you have." Adamant head shake. "Okay, then I have to ask. Why now? You're about to have this baby. What is it you want from him?"

The question seemed to surprise her. "I never asked for any of this. I thought I could do it, have this baby." She shook her head. "He did this to me. He owes me. At the very least he shouldn't threaten me. He needs to admit what he did and take responsibility for it." Tears filled her eyes. "I don't think I can do this alone."

"Do you know the sex of the baby?" Cat asked, thinking of the baby girl she would be giving birth to soon and raising alone.

Another head shake. "I don't want to know."

"Are you thinking about giving the baby up?" More tears and no answer.

Cat could see how conflicted the woman was—and with good reason if what she'd told her was true. The father of the baby had threatened her. If he was the man who'd drugged her and impregnated her, then he could

be dangerous and there might be real malice behind the
threat.

She pulled out her notebook and picked up her pen.
"What's the man's name?"

Chapter Two

When Cat had been offered the job, she hadn't quibbled or even asked a lot of questions. That her first law enforcement job was in the middle of nowhere was perfect. It was wild country, only a few camps along the only highway that followed the Yaak River. Otherwise, it was just mountains and pines, lots of pines.

She hadn't cared that the closest real town was Eureka, miles away, across the narrow Lake Koocanusa that crossed the border into Canada. She was exactly where she'd wanted to be.

She wondered if Dylan Walker felt the same way as she headed south of town toward the ranch Dylan had purchased almost a year ago, but apparently had only moved full time to the ranch three months ago. He'd paid a small fortune for the large, remote, exclusive ranch a dozen miles from Fortune Creek.

From what Cat had learned about the man, he was a thirty-seven-year-old retired construction consultant who had worked abroad much of his career. His former address was in the DC area. He had no social media presence, had apparently never been arrested, and other than a short marriage, had left little to no paper trail.

She could find no photograph of the man other than the poor quality mugshot on his Montana driver's license.

What was interesting was that nine months ago he'd lost his wife in a car bombing in DC following a charity event that they had attended. The same event where Lindsey Martin swore he'd impregnated her. Nine months. There seemed to be a pattern here, Cat told herself.

After getting the pertinent information about the night in question from Ms. Martin, Cat suggested the woman get a room at the Fortune Creek Hotel across the street from the sheriff's office. "You'll be safe there. I'll let you know what I find out," she promised.

Now, as Cat drove the narrow, winding, seldom-used road south through thick pines toward the posted and gated entrance into the isolated ranch, she wondered about the man she'd come to see.

If what Lindsey had told her was true, Dylan Walker probably wasn't going to talk to her either—not without a warrant. This trip was a fact-finding mission. She had to make at least an attempt to talk to the man before she could go to a judge. But with only a threatening note, she doubted she could get a warrant.

As Cat drove up to the unmanned gate, a camera lens followed her every movement as she approached what appeared to be an intercom system. She pulled out her badge and held it out the patrol SUV window, not sure if the camera would pick it up before pressing the intercom button. "Acting Sheriff Cat… Catherine Jameson to see Dylan Walker."

For a moment, she thought she wouldn't get an answer. Then a deep male voice demanded, "What's this about?"

"I need to speak to Dylan Walker about a law enforcement matter," she said.

"You have a warrant?"

"I just need to ask a few questions, but if you insist, I'll get a warrant." She waited, expecting she was going to get the same reception Lindsey Martin had, when she heard the gate clank and begin to slide open.

Relieved and yet wary, she drove in before the gate swung closed behind her. Why all the security? It seemed overkill. Maybe the man had more to hide than even Lindsey Martin knew. Then she reminded herself that his wife had died in a car bombing. Maybe he had reason to fear for his own life.

Before driving out here, she'd read as much as she could find on the car bombing in DC. Lindsey Martin claimed she'd been at the same fundraiser gala as Dylan Walker—the same night as the car bombing. While Cat doubted one had anything to do with the other…it was an interesting coincidence.

Also, it brought up all kinds of questions. If Dylan and his wife, Ginny Cooper Walker, had been together at the event, how did he find time to slip away with Lindsey Martin? Also, how was it that his wife had died and not him? Had they taken separate cars? Or was he busy possibly drugging and then taking advantage of Ms. Martin? Had the bomb been intended for both husband and wife? If so, why would anyone want to kill them? And where did Lindsey Martin fit in all this—if she did.

Cat drove along a narrow road through the thick pines until the trees finally opened up and she caught glimpses of the ranch house. The first word that came to mind was opulent and massive. Stone, giant timbers and walls of

glass rose to three stories and stretched across the landscape directly ahead.

Off to one side was a five-car garage constructed of
the same materials. She noted a small cottage some distance away. The sprawling three-story mansion made
it look like a dollhouse. There was no sign of anyone
around except for a large black SUV parked in front of
the smaller dwelling.

As Cat drove closer, a man came out of the cottage
and stood, hands on his hips, watching her from the front
deck. He wore a flannel shirt, jeans and boots, no hat.
Her first thought was that he must be the caretaker. He
was tall, broad-shouldered, imposing, his stance impatient as he raked a hand through hair that gleamed in
the sunlight and curled at his collar.

She felt suddenly uneasy, her reaction to the man
a surprise. There was no way this was the man of the
manor, was there? *Dylan Walker?*

DYLAN MOVED SWIFTLY to the patrol SUV, planning to
make this as painless and quick as possible. He regret-
ted letting in the local law. But he had to know what
this was about and nip it in the bud. He'd moved here
to disappear. He didn't want attention called to him—
especially by some *acting* sheriff. Better to get this out
of the way and be done with it. Whatever this was.

Before he could reach the patrol SUV, a small, slim
woman climbed out. It wasn't until she turned that he
realized she was pregnant. She wore jeans, a tan short-
sleeved shirt with a silver star on it and a Stetson over
fire-engine red long curly hair that seemed to be fighting
to free itself from the elastic around her low ponytail.

He hadn't gotten a good look at her on the gate sur-veillance camera, so it wasn't until she turned to him that he saw her face beneath the shaded brim of her hat. He'd never seen so many freckles. Nor had she made any attempt to cover them with makeup.

Struck by how young she looked, fresh-faced with a no-nonsense nose and a generous mouth, he found him-self fighting a smile. He couldn't imagine anyone wear-ing a silver star looking more harmless—until he met her eyes. They were an intense blue like the sky overhead. But it was the way those eyes bore into him that sent his pulse racing. There was intelligence there, a sharp mind, and a whole lot of determination mixed with suspicion. What-ever this woman was doing here, she meant business.

"Acting Sheriff Cat… Catherine Jameson," she said again, holding out her hand to shake his. He was looking at her left hand and the plain gold band on it.

Her grip was firm. As they shook hands, she studied him as if looking for something. It felt like she could see into his soul, and he didn't like that feeling. "I need to ask you a few questions. Maybe we should step in-side your house." She glanced toward the larger of the structures.

"That's not my house."

She raised a fine pale brow, those deep blue eyes nar-rowing a little.

"It's my house, but it isn't where I live." He definitely didn't like the way she was looking at him. "What's this about?"

CAT COULD SEE that she wasn't going to be invited inside even the small cottage. Okay, if he wanted to do this out here, she was fine with it. She'd get right to it. "I'm here about a woman named Lindsey Martin."

He frowned, furrowing his brows, making his light blue eyes narrow under brows as dark as his espresso brown hair. "I don't know anyone by that name."

She noticed that he definitely needed a haircut and had for a while now. A lock had fallen over his forehead. He brushed it back with obvious irritation as if he normally wore it much shorter. He also needed a shave, his strong jaw bristled and dark.

"Ms. Martin claims that the two of you met in Washington, DC, about nine months ago."

The nine months seemed to make his eyes darken even further. "If we met, I have no memory of it."

"She claims you had a one-night stand at a gala after drugging her and not using protection, which left her pregnant." He started to interrupt, but she continued. "After she recently contacted you, she also has what appears to be evidence that you threatened her and the baby."

Dylan Walker's face clouded over. She could see him fighting to rein in his anger. He lifted a large, suntanned hand, took a couple of deep breaths and said calmly, "I can assure you that I didn't impregnate anyone—let alone drug and assault a woman I've never heard of. She is mistaken."

"She claims she came out here to the ranch yesterday morning, but that you wouldn't let her in, denied everything, and after that she received a death threat for both her and her baby if she kept causing you trouble. Are you telling me that a woman didn't contact you at your gate yesterday?" she asked. "And you refused to let her in?"

He frowned. "When was this?"

"About 8:00 a.m."

"I take a long ride every morning—just as I did yesterday. There is no way she talked to me."

"Who would she have spoken with then, if not you?"

Letting out a sigh, he said, "I had a guest here. She must have spoken with the woman, though she didn't mention it to me."

"That's odd since Ms. Martin indicated it was a man's voice on the intercom, a man she assumed was you," Cat said.

He shook his head. "I don't know what I can tell you. Like I said, I wasn't here and the only other person on the ranch was Rowena."

"Rowena? I'm going to need her full name and a number where I can reach her." She pulled out her notebook and pen and waited.

"Rowena Keeling." He spelled both names and she wrote them down. "I don't know her cell number. I'll have her call you."

Cat raised a brow. "She's still staying with you?"

He didn't look sure. "I believe she went into Eureka. I'll ask her for her number when she gets back." Apparently, he and his guest weren't very close if he really didn't have her number.

"Ms. Martin left her information about where she was staying in Eureka on a note in your mailbox. Do you still have it?"

He raked a hand through his hair irritably. "I never had it. Maybe Rowena does. I can ask."

Cat studied him, wondering why his guest would take something from his mailbox. Also wondering if he really was the wrong man. He was smooth, controlled and came off as if blindsided by the accusation. She tried to decide if she believed him or the terrified pregnant woman who'd come to her for help.

What would motivate Lindsey Martin to lie? The obvious reason was money. Walker appeared to have a lot of it. Was it possible Lindsey had cooked this up to try to cash in?

But there was one surefire way to prove that Dylan Walker was the father of her baby—a DNA test.

"You do understand that once the baby is born and a DNA sample is taken, the truth will come out," Cat said.

"I certainly hope so because whoever this woman is, she isn't having my baby."

"You're certain?"

"Positive."

Cat wasn't sure what to think. Dylan Walker sounded convinced that a DNA test would prove he wasn't the father of Lindsey Martin's baby. But the fact that they were both in the same place at the same time at a fundraiser gala for an art center nearly nine months ago made even the rookie cop in her suspicious. One of them was lying.

She thought about Lindsey's answers to her questions. Why hadn't she called the police if she really thought she'd been drugged? Because she couldn't be sure. She'd had a lot to drink and the sex had been consensual, she'd said.

All of that could be true. How the pieces fit together—if they did—was beyond Cat at this point. Was it possible Lindsey was mistaken about the man who she claimed had impregnated her?

"Ms. Martin claims she met you the night of an art gala," Cat said.

He shook his head. "Like I said, I don't know anyone by that name. I met a lot of people at the galas. I didn't sleep with any of them."

"The accusations against you are serious, if true."

"I'm aware of that." Dropping his gaze, he shoved aside that errant lock of dark hair. As he did, his fingers absently traced the half-moon scar at his temple as if it was something he often did. Had he been injured that night in the bombing? A muscle tensed in his jaw as he ground out, "I was at an art gala at the same time as your victim, but she's mistaken about me being with her. I was with my wife."

But not all night, Cat thought but hesitated to bring up the bombing or his deceased wife. Clearly, they hadn't been together at the time of the bombing. "You'd be willing to take a DNA test if it comes to that?"

His look confirmed that he was losing his patience. "If it comes to that. But it's a waste of your time, I can assure you. I wasn't the man."

Cat heard pain in his words. She could tell he was regretting opening his gate and letting her in. So why had he talked to her without his lawyer present? Because he really had nothing to hide? Maybe he thought he could convince her of his innocence.

The thing was he kind of had, she realized. She believed him. Or maybe just wanted to believe him. Dylan Walker appeared to be a grieving man in a great deal of emotional pain. He'd bought this ranch before the bombing. Had he planned to live here with his wife at some point? Cat got the impression that he wanted to be alone, and from what she could tell, he was. Except for a woman named Rowena Keeling.

"I'd like to speak to Ms. Keeling." She glanced at the large house where he said he didn't live. Is that where she was staying or in this cottage with him? "When do you expect her back?"

He shook his head. "I have no idea. I'll tell her to call you if I see her. I'm sorry. I don't have her cell phone number. She was a friend of my wife's."

"If you see her, you might want to also ask her for the note Ms. Martin left in your mailbox." When he didn't respond, she added truthfully, "I hope I won't have to come back," as she put away her notebook and pen.

"So do I, Acting Sheriff *Cat* Jameson." His gaze met hers and she felt a shiver run the length of her spine at both his look and the intimacy of calling her by her nickname after her slip-up. Dylan Walker was a very attractive man—in a dark kind of way, but when his gray-eyed gaze softened and he looked at her like that... She had a feeling that he was used to getting what he wanted, she thought with another chill. Right now, he just wanted her gone.

Climbing back into her patrol SUV, she drove around the loop past the big house. It appeared to be empty. No car out front. No sign of anyone else on the property, but with a ranch this size, it would be impossible to know for sure.

She glanced back. Dylan Walker no longer stood outside. If her visit had upset him, he hadn't shown it. Because he wasn't afraid of some acting sheriff out of Fortune Creek, Montana?

She headed for the road out, the gate opening as she

approached. She glanced toward the security camera that followed her departure, wondering if he was watching or if he'd already put all of this out of his mind. She made a mental note to see about getting footage from the surveillance camera that would prove Lindsey Martin had come out here and tried to see him. It could also prove that he was lying about not having spoken with her.

But for now, there was nothing more that she could do until she had enough proof to get a warrant. Cat was more anxious than ever to talk to Lindsey Martin again.

Chapter Three

Dylan stepped into the cottage, closing the door behind him as he swore. What had Rowena been thinking answering his intercom, let alone turning someone away and not even mentioning it to him? Add to that she'd apparently taken a note from his mailbox?

It made him even more suspicious as to why she was here. He couldn't shake the feeling she was waiting for something. Or was it *someone*? He hated being this distrustful, but then again, his deceased wife's former friend had always made him feel like that. Too bad he hadn't been more distrustful of his wife. Maybe then he wouldn't have looked like such a fool when the truth came out.

He went into his small study, swung a shelf of books aside to reveal the safe and opened it. Inside, he took out the phone, unable to shake the foreboding feeling he'd had the moment the acting sheriff had shown up. He saw that he had a message.

Instantly, he knew there was trouble. Only two people had this number and one of them was dead.

Hurriedly, he listened to the message. *Disturbing news. Allen Zimmerman. Cops have ruled it an apparent suicide. Watch your back.*

His pulse jumped, heart dropping. Dylan swore and hurriedly put the phone back before quickly closing the safe and replacing the shelf of books. There was no way Allen had killed himself. No possible way. This had to be because of the rumored leak he'd been warned about.

Feeling shaken, he walked back out to the living room to find Rowena pouring herself a drink. He glanced back at his open study door. Had she heard the voicemail? He felt anger race through his veins like hot lava.

"I didn't hear you buzz to get in the gate," he said, drawing on training he'd been trying hard to forget. "Nor did I hear you drive up." Never show anger or any other emotion when confronting a suspected enemy. Never show your hand—until you're ready.

She turned toward him and smiled. "I didn't buzz in. I got your passcode from your groundskeeper. I didn't want to bother you."

"You've certainly made yourself at home," he commented, keeping both his concern and his irritation at bay—at least for the moment. "I need your cell phone number."

She beamed at that as if she thought he might call her for a date and told him her number, which he wrote down. "Make you a drink?" she asked still smiling as she finished making one for yourself.

"Thanks, but I'm fine."

"Suit yourself," she said as she sighed and made her way to one of his deep leather chairs. She dropped into it and kicked off her heels.

Dylan Walker hadn't wanted company. He'd certainly not invited anyone to his ranch—especially the woman who'd shown up.

"I have to ask, what are you still doing here, Rowena?" He'd been caught off guard when she'd showed up at his gate and he'd foolishly let her in.

"How can you even ask that?" she said with a laugh as she flipped her blond bob. "I'm worried about you. Ginny would have wanted me to make sure you were all right."

Ginny. He hated to even hear his deceased wife's name on this woman's lips—even if Rowena still called herself Ginny's best friend. He couldn't imagine what Ginny had seen in her, but as it turned out he didn't know either woman—his bride or her alleged best friend— very well.

During his short marriage, Ginny had a lot of friends from different walks of life. She'd never had trouble keeping them at arm's length if she didn't care for them. That's why Rowena had been such a surprise, especially when she kept turning up at their house, at parties at other friends, at fundraisers. He'd wondered what Ginny saw in Rowena, who wore her wealth like a lot of people Ginny had known—and disliked.

"I'm fine, so you need not have worried—let alone come all this way," Dylan assured her.

Rowena raised a finely shaped brow, her lips tilting up in a smile that didn't seem to reach her green eyes. "I thought you'd be glad to see me." She glanced around. "I would think you'd get lonely out here all by yourself." She took a sip of her drink, looking relaxed, too relaxed.

She was beautiful, rich and privileged. Like him, she'd apparently grown up in the rarified air of a Manhattan high-rise penthouse, summered abroad or jetted with friends to exclusive locations. Surprisingly, his path

had never intersected with Rowena until Rowena and
Ginny had become friends.

He studied her for a moment, remembering the day
she'd been the one at the gate wanting to be let in. That
had been four days ago. He'd been more than surprised
to see her. She'd said she was passing through Montana.
People didn't pass through Montana, not unless they
were coming from Chicago or Seattle or on a backroad
to Canada.

Dylan had called her on it, and she'd admitted that
she'd come to see his ranch. Another lame excuse. "You
know how close Ginny and I were. She would have
wanted me to check up on you."

He wasn't sure about either of those answers. Rowena
was the only one who said she and Ginny were best
friends. He'd often thought the friendship was one-sided,
so why had Ginny let Rowena cling to her like she had?

Shaking his head, he realized he'd let her do the same
thing. When he'd let her in the gate, he'd thought she'd be
gone by morning. Just passing through, like she said. So
why was she still here, and why was he letting her stay?

"What are you *really* doing here?" he asked as he sat
down on the edge of the chair across from her and leaned
forward to rest his elbows on his knees.

"I beg your pardon?"

"It's a valid question."

Rowena gave him an irritated look. "I told you. I
wanted to see your ranch I heard you'd bought." She
sighed. "I also wanted to see how you were doing. It
hasn't even been a year since Ginny died."

"Do you really think you need to remind me how
long ago it was that my wife was murdered?" he de-

manded as he pushed to his feet. "And no, I don't want to talk about it."

"Maybe you should," she said. "Have you talked to anyone about it?" He mugged a face in answer. "Don't you think you need to deal with all of it?"

"I just told you I don't want to talk about it. Let's talk about your life. What happened to your last relationship, which number was he?"

She rose as well. "You're just being spiteful now."

Dylan didn't want to take out his frustration on this woman. But what was she doing here? Surely she didn't have romantic designs on him. She wasn't that clueless.

"The sheriff was here wanting to talk to you," he said, watching her. "I just texted her office your number."

"I saw her. Wasn't she just cute as a button?" The use of the phrase made her sarcasm irritate him even more. "And pregnant!" She laughed.

"How do you know she was pregnant unless…" He stared at her. "You were parked close by watching her?" *Watching me*, he thought.

"I waited until she left," she said. "Why would she want to talk to me?"

"She wanted to know about a visitor I apparently had at my gate while I was out horseback riding yesterday morning," he said.

"A visitor?" She took a sip of her drink.

He glared at her. "Apparently you failed to mention it."

"Oh, that deluded woman? I wasn't about to let her in. I really couldn't understand anything she was saying."

"Probably made it easier to find out what was going on when you read the note you saw her leave in my mailbox."

Rowena froze for a moment, then sighed. "It was all nonsense, I couldn't make heads nor tails out of—"

"I want to see the note."

She blinked then finished her drink. She stood and walked to the bar to make herself another one. "I threw it away."

"Did she mention on the note that she was pregnant?"

"Do you think that was her problem?" Rowena asked, turning to look at him wide-eyed. "Must be something that's catching up here in these parts."

"I'm serious."

She waved a hand through the air as if swatting away a pesky fly. "What does it matter?"

"Maybe it's nothing," he admitted. "The sheriff just had a few questions. But you've only made things more difficult for me."

"If it makes you happy, I'll talk to the sheriff when she calls." She looked at him, brow raised, as she walked to her chair with her fresh drink. "Is this all that has you so upset? I thought it was because you'd heard the news out of DC."

He looked at her in surprise, almost expecting her to tell him about Allen Zimmerman, his old boss, except she shouldn't know anything or anyone from that world. She'd been the rich divorcee who moved in next door and became friends with his wife. The party girl who he'd often found finishing off a second or third bottle of wine in the afternoon with Ginny while he'd been at work.

"I was afraid it would upset you when you heard that they were reopening the car bombing investigation that killed our Ginny," she said, making a sad face.

Our Ginny? At least she was smart enough not to

mention his brother, Beau, who just happened to be in the car with her when it exploded. "Where did you hear they were reopening the case?"

"A friend who works in the prosecutor's office. Maybe they'll finally find the person who did it and you'll get closure. That is why you moved way out here, wasn't it? To forget?"

"Did your friend say why they were reopening the case?" he asked.

"No, they're being really hush-hush about it," she said and shrugged. "I do wonder why."

So did he. He realized he did want that drink. At the bar, he found he was anything but calm now. "Does the name Lindsey Martin mean anything to you?" he asked as he poured some bourbon into a glass.

"No, should it? Who is she?"

"The woman who'd tried to get in yesterday, the one you turned away, the one whose note you destroyed," he said and took a gulp of his drink. "But you wouldn't know anything about that, right?"

"Really, Dylan," she said as she rose to join him at the bar. She stood so close that he could feel the heat coming off her well-toned body. She dropped her voice and asked seductively, "Whatever are you accusing me of?"

He'd felt uneasy before Rowena had shown up at his door and then the acting sheriff. He couldn't believe Zimmerman was dead and now this news about the bombing case being reopened? Trouble often seemed to hitch a ride on an ill wind, as his brother Beau used to say. Rowena, he suspected, like his dead brother, was that ill wind.

He'd thought he'd left that life behind him when he'd

moved to Montana. Clearly, he'd been wrong. His past was coming for him and anyone who got in the way—like the acting sheriff, he thought with a curse—could be in the line of fire.

"Are you in some kind of trouble, Dylan?"

Turning toward Rowena, he smiled and dropped his voice just as she had done. "Seriously, I think you've accomplished whatever it is you've come here for."

"You're wrong about that," she said, almost sounding sad. "Would you mind terribly if I stayed just a few more days? I've come all this way. There are some things I want to see while I'm out here. I promise to stay out of your way, if you don't mind me remaining in the main house that long."

He wasn't sure why he did it. Because it wasn't that much to ask? Or because it would give him time to try to find out what Rowena was really doing out here. "A few days, but no more. I'm sorry, but I need this time alone. That's why I bought this place."

"I understand," she said. "I know how much you loved Ginny and she loved you." He nodded, even though it was hard to do so. Not everyone knew about Ginny's betrayal—or his brother's. "I'll be gone by the weekend," she promised and moved to kiss his cheek. "Thank you," she whispered next to his ear.

With that, she left, leaving behind the scent of her perfume. He watched her walk over to the main house and disappear inside as he locked the cottage door behind her and went into the study. He reminded himself to change the passcode on the gate as soon as she was gone.

But right now, he desperately needed to find out what

was going on. Why would there be something new in the almost year-old bombing case now?

BACK IN FORTUNE CREEK, Cat went straight to the hotel across the street from the sheriff's department. The entire town was only a few blocks long, with an old hotel, a general store with a gas station, a bar and a sheriff's office. The main drag dead-ended at the creek. She'd been shocked that there was even a sheriff's department here at all. But it was the only law in this part of northwestern Montana, only miles from the Canadian border.

The hotel was a four-story narrow building that was being restored after years of remaining empty. Former high school and NFL football star Ash Hammond had returned to town to buy the hotel after a career-changing injury. He was behind the counter when she walked in. Young and good-looking with dark-hair and a ready smile, Ash greeted her cheerfully.

He'd been one of the few people who had welcomed her with open arms. Most of the locals preferred Sheriff Brandt Parker and made no bones about it, even when she pointed out that she was only acting sheriff until he returned.

"Beautiful day, isn't it?" Ash said smiling. "I was just about to head up the street to get some lunch." His options were limited for lunch—the café or the convenience mart. "Want to join me?"

"Thanks, but I need to speak with one of your guests, Lindsey Martin. What room did you put her in?" she asked as she started for the stairs. The old elevator had been refurbished, but she needed to get her steps in.

"In 307, except she isn't there," Ash said. "Checked

her in, took her bags up and the next thing I knew the elevator opened and there she was with her bags saying she couldn't stay."

"She checked out?" Cat couldn't keep the incredulity out of her tone. She'd told the woman that she'd be safe here in Fortune Creek—especially staying right across the street from the sheriff's department. "Did she say why she was leaving?" Ash shook his head. "Did she at least say where she was going?" Another shake of his head. "Surely she left me a message." He'd already started to shake his head before she said, "Any chance she went across the street to my office?"

"Sorry. I carried her bags out to her vehicle, she got behind the wheel and left."

Was it possible she'd gotten another threat? Cat wondered. One that had scared her away? "What was her general demeanor?"

Ash shrugged. "Maybe a little anxious to be on her way, but she wasn't acting scared, if that's what you're thinking. She just seemed to have changed her mind."

About the hotel room or about her allegations against Dylan Walker? Cat wondered as she headed back across the street to her office. As she did, she saw a vehicle drive in and park in front of the hotel. She stopped to watch two men dressed in business attire climb out of an SUV.

She watched the larger of the two look around, his gaze lighting on her and the small sheriff's department building before he turned and the two disappeared inside the hotel. The men couldn't have looked more out of place, which made her wonder what had brought them to Fortune Creek.

Definitely not tourists, not this time of the year, she thought, as she made her way to her office and put the two men out of her mind—at least temporarily as she hoped Lindsey Martin and her baby were okay. As pregnant as Lindsey had been, maybe she'd decided she needed to be closer to a hospital.

The entire Fortune Creek, Montana, sheriff's office was matchbox size, with only Cat and Helen holding down the fort, so to speak. As uneventful as things had been in town since she'd taken over, Cat wondered how Helen spent her days—let alone how the sheriff did. Given the amount of knitted throws the elderly woman had produced in the short time Cat had been there, she had a pretty good idea at least how Helen filled her time in the office.

As Cat walked in, still worried and confused about Lindsey Martin's quick exit, she found Helen knitting—of course. The older woman barely looked up as the acting sheriff approached her desk. "By any chance did the pregnant woman from earlier call and leave me a message?"

Helen didn't look up from her knitting. "Called. In your office on your desk."

"Thank you." Trying not to sigh, she went to her desk. The message was written in Helen's neat cursive. *Lindsey Martin: I changed my mind.* The time and date were written after it. Lindsey had called the office with the message shortly after Cat had left town to talk to Dylan Walker.

Sticking her head out her door, she asked, "Did you get a phone number from her?"

"Called from the hotel right after you left."

Back in her office, she glared at Helen through the office window, saying to herself, "Would have been nice to know on my way out to see Dylan Walker." Helen didn't look up, which was probably just as well. Cat wondered how she could ever get the woman to quit treating her like an outsider. For that matter, it was the same with a lot of the residents of the town. It wasn't just that they liked Brandt Parker better, even though they did. They seemed to question how a woman had gotten the acting sheriff job—especially a pregnant one who, while wearing a wedding ring, clearly didn't have a husband living with her.

Cat figured it was none of their business and definitely *not* something she wanted to talk about. She reminded herself that she only had a few months here. She was determined to make the best of it, as boring and uneventful as the job had turned out to be.

Sitting down at her desk, she did question what she was doing here especially when she didn't seem to be wanted. It wasn't as if she was interested in a popularity contest with the handsome cowboy sheriff Brandt Parker, because she would lose hands down. He was loved and admired and apparently so handsome that some New Yorker named Molly had turned his head, tricked him into marriage and taken him off on some long honeymoon—at least that was the local story. Cat almost felt sorry for the woman she'd never met. This was a rough town to win over. She wondered how Helen had taken it. She guessed not well.

As for the locals wanting to know her story, she saw no reason to share it. She told herself that she wouldn't be here that long. *Let them speculate all they wanted*, she thought as she laid her palm on her stomach. As she felt her baby move, that wonderful flutter she loved, she smiled to herself. This was her story and no one else's.

Turning back to business, she studied the message Lindsey had left. Had the woman gotten cold feet after her get-rich plan hadn't worked? Or had she been threatened again and scared off?

Cat balled up the message and chucked it into the trash. She reached for the notes she'd started with the complaint against Dylan Walker. She'd asked Lindsey if she wanted to get a restraining order against Walker. She hadn't.

Seeing how scared the woman had been, Cat had figured she'd speak to him first. After that Ms. Martin could decide how she wanted to proceed.

Now that she had talked to Dylan Walker, she wasn't sure who she believed. Lindsey had appeared frightened for herself and her baby. Dylan had seemed straightforward in his responses with nothing to hide. Which one was telling the truth?

A thought struck her. Could Lindsey have been faking the pregnancy with a cushion under her clothes hoping to shake down the apparently wealthy Walker?

But if she was truly having his baby, why change her mind? Cold feet?

Cat thought about calling him to let him know that the woman had changed her mind. But he'd said he didn't know a woman by that name, and he hadn't seemed worried that it would go any further than it had. Also, he'd been willing to prove that he wasn't the father of the baby—if it came to that.

She jotted a couple of notes down, retrieved Lindsey's note from the trash, flattened it out and put it in a file folder in case the woman returned. At least it had been a break in the monotony that was Fortune Creek law enforcement, she told herself.

Maybe she should ask Helen to teach her to knit, she thought, watching the blur of needles in the woman's hands. Might be a way to bond—and not go mad for the rest of the time she had left as acting sheriff.

Then again, could she trust that Helen wouldn't "accidently" jab her with a knitting needle?

Chapter Four

The call came in the middle of the night—two days after Cat met Lindsey Martin and Dylan Walker.

She'd been in the middle of a dream where she was drowning and couldn't seem to kick to the surface. Fighting her way out of the twisted sheets, she sat up gasping for breath to find the phone ringing. Her heart still pumping hard, she struggled to breathe. As she put her hand on her stomach, she looked around the small upstairs apartment over the Fortune Creek Sheriff's Office, trying to assure herself that she was safe—and so was her baby.

It had just been a bad dream. Except that it had felt so real. Snatching up her phone, the dream slipped back into her unconscious ether-land. "Acting Sheriff Catherine Jameson," she said, her voice sounding as shaky as she felt. Maybe the nightmare hadn't gone completely away.

"There's a body on the side of the road a mile out of town," a male voice told her. "Looks like a young woman. Thought you'd want to know."

She took down the rancher's name, the mile marker on the road where he'd pulled over, told him she'd be right there and called the coroner.

Twenty minutes later, dressed and armed, Cat stood

on the side of the road. Coroner JP Brown was already down in the ditch hunkered over the body. He'd beaten her to the scene after her urgent call since he lived closer and probably dressed faster, Cat thought. He was already taking photos when she arrived.

Since he seemed to know what he was doing, she let him continue. She'd been trying not to step on anyone's toes after taking the temporary job. She'd been warned about JP Brown. Helen wasn't the only one who wanted Sheriff Brandt Parker back and Cat long gone. It was as if she wore a sign around her neck: Just Out of the Academy. Add Pregnant and it was no wonder some just assumed she wasn't up to the job.

The worst part? It was true. She was green, and this was her first baby and her first law enforcement job at the ripe old age of thirty-two. Wasn't that why she'd gotten this gig? Nothing ever happened in Fortune Creek, Montana, right? Even she should be able to handle filling in for the sheriff for a few months before she was to give birth.

The bite of the wind warned that the weather had changed. In this part of Montana that could mean anything, even snow any month of the year. But it was late fall so all bets were off when the first snow would hit. Often once flakes did hit the ground, they remained until April, and sometimes May.

From where she stood, Cat could tell the body in the ditch was slim and female. "Think she was hit by a vehicle?" Cat asked, hugging herself against the cold. The woman was curled up almost protectively, her back to the road, most of her head covered by the hoodie she wore.

Coroner JP Brown looked up from where he was

crouched down by the body and shook his head. "Shot.
Looks like a .38 to the heart. Three times at close range."
He yelled up to his van, telling a young assistant huddled
in the passenger seat to get the body bag and cart ready.

"Mind if I take a look first?" Cat said. JP Brown was
a large older man who'd grown up in Montana, collected
guns and spent his free time killing things. He fished
year around, hunted during the seasons and did taxi-
dermy in between being called out as coroner. He'd been
married a couple of times and then had stayed single saying he hadn't found a woman who could put up with him.

That he had little patience with most people, law enforcement even less, was well known around the state.
That he especially had no patience with green acting
sheriffs was the first thing Cat had been warned about.

Flashlight in hand, she stepped off the side of the road
and dropped down into the steep ditch, sliding partway
down to where the body had come to rest. From the lack
of blood in the grass as she slid, Cat guessed the woman
hadn't been killed here. "Dumped?"

JP didn't bother to answer.

She moved carefully around the body. "Why three
shots to the heart?" she asked and got only a grunt from
the coroner. Seemed like overkill to Cat, but apparently,
he wasn't interested in discussing it.

From what she could see in the beam of her flashlight, the woman was slim, wearing sweats, a hooded
sweatshirt, no shoes. The bottoms of her bare feet were
clean. She'd definitely been killed somewhere else and
dropped here.

"Find an ID?" she asked.

"Nope."

"Why dump her so close to town and right beside the road?" This was Montana. There were miles and miles of places to hide a body where it might never be found. "It almost seems as if the killer wanted her to be found. Or wasn't able to carry her far."

No response. Cat hunkered down to move the hoodie back. A lock of long brunette hair fell across the woman's cheek. Cat felt a jolt of recognition. "*I know her. She came into my office two days ago.*" She moved the flashlight down the woman's body and felt suddenly sick to her stomach as she let out a gasp. "Where's her baby? She was very pregnant, looked as if she might give birth at any moment." Cat looked up at the coroner. *"Where's the baby?"*

"You're sure there was a baby?" he asked.

Cat had already questioned that herself, especially since the woman hadn't stuck around after making her accusation. What if the whole thing had been a scam? "I'm not sure," she admitted. "She certainly looked pregnant. But she did claim that someone wanted to kill her and her baby and now she's dead—and the baby's missing."

"*If* there *was* a baby," JP said. "Better get her to the morgue and find out."

HAD IT ALL been a ruse? But to what end? She almost hoped it was true because she couldn't bear the thought that there was a baby out there missing or maybe dead. The woman had definitely acted pregnant. Cat had bought it—until the woman took off saying she'd changed her mind. She couldn't believe that she'd fallen for Lindsey Martin's story—if that was even really her name—and that she'd made it all up. Now Cat doubted everything the woman had told her.

Back in her office after a preliminary search of the highway near where the body was found, Cat opened the temporary file she'd started on the woman. She put everything she'd learned into a computer file. There wasn't much to add so far. She was waiting for a call from JP, needing to know whether or not the woman had been pregnant.

In the meantime, Cat went online to find there were dozens of Lindsey Martins, but none of them were the woman who'd come crying into the Fortune Creek Sheriff's Office.

No social media. Also, no record of a Lindsey Martin her age living in the Denver area. Either that or she'd lived off the grid, no television, no internet, no electricity, no water, no sewage, no taxes, no driver's license, no purchase of anything that left a paper trail.

How was that even possible? Because that Lindsey Martin had never existed. The woman had lied about everything except, she reminded herself, someone wanting to kill her. Once they had her prints, maybe they would find out who she was—let alone if she'd been pregnant. And if true, who might have killed her. She kept thinking about how frightened the woman had been that Dylan Walker was going to kill her and her baby. So why hadn't she stayed at the hotel so Cat could have tried to keep her safe? Where had she gone after she left Fortune Creek? Out to Walker's ranch again?

Her phone rang. "Acting Sheriff Catherine Jameson," she said quickly.

"She'd recently given birth," JP said without preamble. So, there was a baby! "It was a live birth."

Cat had been warned not to ask JP a lot of questions. Not that it stopped her. "How can you tell that?"

"She breastfed the baby before she was killed."

"You can tell that?" Cat felt physically ill at the thought of the missing baby. She'd been hoping that the woman had been a scam artist, that there hadn't been a baby. Now she had a dead woman and a missing baby. Had the killer taken it? Dumped the infant along the road miles before dumping the mother's body? Was the baby even still alive?

Her hand went to her own baby bump as she rose quickly from her desk, phone still in hand. "We need to organize a search party along the road and—"

"Already did it at first light," JP said. "Covered all the miles from Eureka to Fortune Creek. No baby."

"Thank you," Cat said, even though she wished he'd let her know about the search. Clearly, he didn't think she was capable of helping.

Admittedly, she felt she hadn't handled things well so far. The woman was dead, her baby missing. But short of locking Lindsey Martin in a cell, she didn't know how she could have protected her. She'd thought she would be safe at the hotel across the street, but the woman had bolted on her.

"You're sure her name was Lindsey Martin?" JP asked.

"That's what she told me," Cat said, hating that the woman's purse was missing. There would have been a driver's license in it.

"Wait," the coroner said. "She showed you her identification when she came in to file a complaint, right?"

"No." *Novice.* She could hear the coroner echoing her sentiments. "She hesitated about filing a written complaint so I told her we could do it after I verified her story. I talked to the man in question, planning to talk to her again but she'd taken off."

He grunted.

She couldn't argue that. Why hadn't she asked for identification? Because she tended to take people at face value. "I do have the threatening note she said she received. Her fingerprints will be on it. I'm waiting to hear back from DCI's crime lab. They'll be trying to get prints off the note."

"I'll take her prints and send them to you," JP said.

After she disconnected, she thought that maybe Ash over at the hotel had asked for the woman's ID. She quickly called.

"Sorry, she paid cash. When I told her I'd need a credit card for incidentals, she told me she had one in her other purse in her suitcase and would bring it down later. Maybe that's why she split because there wasn't another purse—let alone a credit card in the name she'd given you."

Yep, that was pretty much what Cat was thinking. She thanked him and got off the call so she could start contacting hospitals, motels and hotels to see if a baby had been born there last night. The hospital would have required more information from her than Cat had gotten. She had no idea where Lindsey Martin had gone, let alone where she might have given birth. Maybe she knew someone in the area and felt safer staying with them, although that hadn't seemed the case. Or she gave birth in the motel in Eureka where she'd been staying. That was the problem, Cat had no idea. But she had to do something to find that baby.

"I'm going to alert the newspapers and radio stations in the two closest towns, Eureka and Libby, as well as the radio and TV stations around the state about the missing baby," Cat told JP when he called.

"Every crackpot in the state will be calling you, but if that's what you think is best." His tone made it clear he didn't think it was best, but Cat was determined.

"The sooner we find the baby, the better."

JP cleared his voice. "If you're going to do it, maybe you should let them know that the missing baby was a boy."

"A boy?" She didn't ask how he knew, just assumed he did. "Glad you agree with my plan," she said. She waited, expecting him to tell her she'd better turn the whole case over to DCI. "I guess I don't have to tell you that this is my first murder."

"Nope. What *was* the story she told you, anyway?"

"Said the father of her baby threatened her and the baby. I spoke with the alleged bio-father. He swore he'd never heard of her and that he hadn't gotten her pregnant—and could prove it if he had to."

"Well, he has to now. Get a warrant now. Call Judge Nicholas Grand."

"Thanks." She really was grateful, feeling that she probably was in over her head and suspecting Helen and JP knew it. And yet neither had said she should call in help. Yet.

"What about the car she was driving?" JP asked. "Did you happen to get the license plate number?"

"No." *Another rookie mistake.* The car was missing. What if the baby was inside? "She told me she drove up from Denver."

"Probably did drive. Flying would be risky so far into her pregnancy," JP said.

"I'll see if there's a car registered to her." Cat said. "If her name really was Lindsey Martin. Otherwise, I'll check flights and car rental agencies."

"Get some of the deputies out of Eureka and Libby to help," he said.

"Also, might want to know that she was about three weeks overdue. It's a wonder she didn't give birth in your office the day she came in to see you. Maybe that's why she left the Fortune Creek Hotel."

"To get help from someone?" He grunted in reply. "Which means she didn't get pregnant at the gala…" she said more to herself than the coroner.

"Hopefully her prints will confirm who she is," JP said. "Sending them to you now."

Cat knew it wouldn't help unless the woman's prints were in the system. She had her fingers crossed as she made the calls to the police chiefs in the two closest cities and got the word out about the missing baby. She just hoped that one of her inquiries would give her the information she needed before she went to the judge for a warrant to search Dylan Walker's ranch for any sign of the crime or the baby. She wasn't looking forward to questioning him again—if he was still on the ranch.

To her surprise, the prints she sent to the IFAIS database got a match at once. They belonged to a woman named Athena Grant, an import-export manager who had worked for several large companies abroad. After a quick check, Cat found that she was nowhere on social media—just like Dylan Walker. She also had no home address or phone number listed in the Denver area.

When Cat dug a little deeper, she found that Athena had only returned to the states three months ago—about the time Dylan Walker moved to his ranch. She called JP back with the news, asked him to send a photograph of Athena, then contacted the judge for a warrant.

Before walking out the door, she made copies of Athena Grant's passport photo and those from JP of the deceased woman lying on his morgue table. Then she called her friend Traver Lee, who she'd known since he roomed with her cousin in college. He now worked for the tabloid. She couldn't shake the feeling that Athena's death tied in somehow to the DC bombing and Dylan Walker and his dead wife.

Chapter Five

On the way to Dylan Walker's ranch, Traver Lee called her back. She picked up immediately, anxious to hear what he'd dug up on the background information she'd given him about on Dylan Walker and the car bombing that killed his wife.

Cat couldn't help being curious about the bombing that had killed Dylan's wife. But after meeting Dylan Walker, she'd been curious about the woman he'd married. Earlier she'd found photos of Ginny Cooper Walker from the bombing story. Dylan's wife had been beautiful, supermodel stunning with long dark hair, huge blue eyes and a body that would stop traffic with those long legs that seemed to go on forever.

"So what do you have for me?" she asked Traver, knowing how he loved digging up dirt. He was apparently exceptionally good at it.

"How much do you know?" he asked, sounding downright gleeful.

"Just what I've been able to find online, which isn't much. I wanted to ask if the husband, Dylan Walker, had been injured in the bombing."

"According to his statement to the cops, he was almost to the town car when it had pulled away from the curb, gone up the street and exploded. He apparently had gone out into the street as if he planned to chase it down when it blew up. The explosion was contained so he received only minor injuries, was taken to the hospital for observation, and released later that night. Everyone in the car was killed instantly, but bystanders were relatively unharmed."

"So, the idea was to kill whoever was in the car," she said. "Wait, you said *everyone* in the car? I thought it was just the wife and driver?"

"Beau Walker was driving the car. Ginny Walker was in the front. Both were killed," he said.

She frowned. "*Beau* Walker?"

"Dylan Walker's younger brother. There were rumors about Beau being with Dylan's wife, Ginny. I never could get verification, but Ginny and Beau had been seen together more than once before that night."

Cat had tried to picture it. Dylan hurrying after the car as it was pulling away. Which meant that he and his wife hadn't been together all night. So much for his alibi. "So, the car bomb wasn't designed to detonate when the car was started?"

"No, it was on a delayed electronic trigger," he said. "The killer was probably either watching from somewhere or had someone else telling them when to detonate the bomb."

"Do the cops know who the actual target was?"

"Nope, the case has never been solved," he said.

"I'm curious about the wife and brother."

He made a sound of agreement. "Beau Walker worked abroad as an independent contractor on construction projects." Apparently, like his older brother Dylan. "At the time of his death, he was in between jobs. He and his brother both came from old family wealth, I'm talking loaded, and the surviving brother inherited it all." That could definitely have given Dylan motive for murder—not to mention if he suspected his wife and brother were having an affair.

"What do you know about the wife?" she asked, trying to hide just how curious she was.

"Ginny Cooper Walker was playing above her league. Middle-class family and upbringing. BFA after majoring in art. Taught children how to finger paint through a program Dylan's family had started. They met at one of the events. Love at first sight, according to friends."

"The marriage?" she asked.

"True love according to her sister, Patty. Dylan idolized Ginny. But they hadn't been married long. Patty Cooper Harper teaches middle school in Denver."

Denver? Where Lindsey Martin said she was from. Coincidence?

"So why the car bomb?" Cat asked as she made the turn toward the Walker ranch.

"Could have been a case of mistaken identity," he said. "There were a half dozen black town cars hired at the event that night."

Cat thought of Lindsey Martin aka Athena Grant again. "Did the brothers look anything alike?"

Traver laughed. "Odd you should ask, but no more than most brothers. You know something I don't?"

She wasn't about to tell him about the murder case she was working on. He was a reporter and there was no way he could sit on this story. Maybe when she solved the murder, she could give it to him. "You think the bomb was meant for Dylan?"

"I think it had something to do with the brother and Dylan's wife."

"An affair then?" she asked.

"Why not? Makes you wonder why Dylan didn't leave the event with his wife. The rumor is that Dylan didn't even know his brother was in town."

"Were they close?" she asked.

"Wouldn't be very close once Dylan found out that his wife was sleeping with his brother."

"You know that for a fact?" Cat asked.

"Honey, let's not even pretend I work on fact," he said with a laugh. "I just try to answer the questions everyone is asking."

Cat could see the gate ahead and two rigs with the deputies she'd called from Eureka and Libby waiting to help with the search. "I'm going to have to let you go."

"I hope you can tell me soon why you're asking about this now."

"You're the best, Traver," she said with a chuckle and disconnected as she reached the gate.

Cat tried to make sense of what she knew. Athena Grant was more than nine months pregnant and in trouble. She'd come to Montana thinking she could get Dylan Walker to help her. But she had to know that was a longshot. Was that why she hadn't used her real name? Because once he knew it was her, there was no way he would see her? Or worse, what if she planned to kill him if she'd gotten in through the gate that day?

She shook her head, reminding herself that law enforcement operated on facts and evidence, not conjec-

ture and rumor. But right now, conjecture and rumor
was about all she had. She did wonder though if Athena
had had a backup plan. If so, something went wrong.

IT WAS LATE afternoon on Saturday when Dylan looked
out to see Rowena headed his way. She'd said she'd be
gone by the weekend, but here she was. He hadn't seen
much of her over the past few days. She had come and
gone. From what little he'd seen of her, she seemed to be
sightseeing around the area, leaving early in the morning and returning late.

The first words out of her mouth were, "I know what
you're going to say. What am I still doing here." She
gave him a smile. "Make me a drink and I'll tell you."

"Rowena—"

"Seriously, Dylan, you'll want to hear what I have
to tell you. I talked to my friend in the prosecutor's office. Make it a gin and tonic with lime," she said as she
stepped past him.

Tamping down his growing irritation, he closed the
door and followed her into the living room, where she'd
already taken a seat on the couch. He'd done his best to
find out what she was doing here, but none of his contacts
knew anything. That was the problem with Rowena, he
couldn't remember how she'd come into Ginny's life—
and now his own.

Maybe she was just this pushy woman who latched
onto people and hung on for dear life because she didn't
have other friends. Is this what Ginny had had to con-
tend with? Or was Rowena really her best friend, the one
she told all her secrets to? He might never know. The

one thing he did know was that he couldn't get Rowena to tell him the truth.

Dylan made her a drink and one for himself while he was at it. He figured he was going to need it. He handed her a glass, she gave a nod and made herself at home. "Well? Let's have it." He did his best not to sound as angry as he felt as he perched on the arm of the chair across from her. Or as worried. Whatever she was doing here, it was more than to visit him.

His stomach roiled as he watched her take a sip of her drink, lick her lips and carefully put down the glass on the coffee table before she answered. She was making him wait, maybe gauging just how anxious he was to hear what she'd found out. More than likely torturing him for the fun of it. Still, he waited, sipping his drink, trying his best to look calm and casual.

"They've reopened the case because there's some question about who died in the car," she said.

"*What?* After this long there's a question?"

"Something to do with identifying the remains, a possible mix-up."

Dylan shook his head. "I saw Ginny get into the car and head up the street right before it blew up. I provided a sample of my DNA. It was my brother in that car."

Rowena picked up her drink, took a sip before she said, "I don't know what to tell you, but it sounds as if there might have been a major screwup if the people in the car weren't your brother and wife."

"That's impossible."

"Just telling you what I heard. Why else would they reopen the case?" she asked.

He had no idea, but he had a feeling she might be

making this all up since he hadn't been able to confirm the case was being reopened. This could be Rowena playing him. But for what end? So she could hang around longer? But why? Not that it mattered, he was done.

"It's time for you to leave, Rowena."

She raised a brow and let out a little laugh. "It's not even close to bedtime and I'm lonely in that big house of yours. I really don't understand why you don't live in it. You could come stay with me and then it wouldn't be so—"

"Not leave to go back to my house. Leave the ranch. Leave Montana. You said you'd leave by the weekend. Time's up."

Rowena cocked her head at him. He could see sparks coming from her blue eyes as she downed the rest of her drink. "Ginny said I was wrong, but you never liked me, did you, Dylan?"

"No. I never understood what Ginny saw in you."

"Ouch, the gloves are off, huh. I'll tell you what Ginny saw in me. I was fun, something she found in short supply with you." She rose, taking her empty glass to the bar and pouring herself another drink. After downing it in one gulp, she slammed her glass on the bar before turning to him. "I really did come here to help you get over your…loss," she said meeting his gaze with a fiery one of her own.

"I highly doubt that. Did you ever contact the sheriff like I told her you would?"

"*Acting* sheriff," she said, with a shake of her head.

"You should give her a call on your way out of town."

"What makes you think I'm leaving town," she said with a bitter laugh.

"Montana's a big state. There is no reason you and I should cross paths again."

She let out a huff and started for the door but stopped at the sound of the gate buzzer. Turning, they exchanged a look as a familiar female voice came over the intercom.

Dylan swore under his breath. He had feared Acting Sheriff Cat Jameson would be back. Just a gut feeling he hadn't been able to explain. He touched the intercom flat-screen display and her face appeared. "Unless you've brought a warrant, Sheriff—"

"Got it right here, along with some deputies to help with the search."

"Search? Search for what?"

"It's all spelled out in the warrant," she said, holding it up.

He felt his pulse begin to pound. "Come on in then." He opened the gate, dreading what he feared was coming as she drove in followed by two different cars of deputies apparently from nearby cities. What the devil was this about?

Turning back to Rowena, he said, "I need to handle this. I'm serious about you leaving."

"But didn't you tell me the cute little acting sheriff wanted to talk to me?"

He growled under his breath. "That's right. Unfortunately, you involved yourself in this."

She smiled and raised a brow. "Nor would I want to miss this for anything. They're really going to search the place? Seems you're in some kind of trouble, Dylan. Now I'm really intrigued. Whatever have you been up to?"

Chapter Six

Dylan ground his teeth as he waited for the sheriff to reach the house. Worse, he waited with Rowena, wondering how much she already knew since she seemed to be enjoying herself. She'd been the only one around when a woman named Lindsey Martin had tried to get in to see him. She'd not just read the woman's note to him—she'd destroyed it. Why would she do that unless she knew more about what was going on than he did?

He told himself that it didn't matter. It wasn't true and he was about to resolve this once and for all. Although he did wonder how the sheriff had gotten a warrant. Based on what? None of this boded well, he told himself as he heard the vehicles coming up the road.

"Stay here," he told Rowena, who immediately began to pour herself another drink. "Try not to get too drunk."

Going out onto the small bungalow deck, he waited as the sheriff drove up, parked, and two other law enforcement vehicles pulled in next to her.

From her demeanor the moment she set foot on his property, Acting Sheriff Cat Jameson was all business and so were the four deputies she'd brought with her.

"I have a warrant to search your house and property,"

she said as she marched up to him and handed him the folded paper.

He quickly glanced at it, then at her as the deputies scaled the steps to the porch. "You're looking for a *baby*?" Dylan said unable to keep the shock out of his voice.

"While the deputies search your house and property, I need to ask you a few questions on the record," she said. "We can do it here or I can take you to the sheriff's office in Fortune Creek. Your choice."

"Here is fine," he said wondering how this situation had gone this far this fast.

"Shall we step inside then," she said and, hefting the bag she carried, started for the door.

All he could do was nod as the deputies entered the house, the acting sheriff right behind them. Dylan brought up the rear. The warrant had caught him off guard. He'd thought he would be safe out here in Montana on a ranch as big as some towns. He hadn't expected a warrant because he couldn't imagine what judge would give her one without sufficient evidence.

Which meant she'd found evidence that incriminated him—or…the woman who'd implicated him had given birth to her baby—and someone had taken it? Why else would they be searching for a baby?

"Let me save you some time," he said once he and the acting sheriff had stepped into the bungalow's bright, sunny kitchen. He could hear the deputies searching the cottage. He knew it wouldn't take them long since the place was small. Then they would want to search the big house. "There's no baby here."

She pulled out a chair, indicating he should do the

same. With a sigh, he said, "Also my…houseguest, Rowena Keeling, is here. She's the one who must have spoken to the woman who stopped by the ranch. She also was the one who took the note from the mailbox."

As if on cue, Rowena stepped into the doorway. "Before you ask, I don't have the note. The woman sounded irrational and unhinged. I didn't open the gate to let her in and while I did check the mailbox to see if maybe she left a bomb or something, I did find the note and throw it away."

"Excuse me, what is your name?"

"Rowena Keeling."

"Did you read the note?" Cat asked her. Dylan saw her react to the waves of alcohol coming off his so-called houseguest.

"It was chicken scrawl. I couldn't make heads nor tails of it. I just figured she had the wrong house and tossed it." Rowena shrugged. "If that's all, I've had a long day." She turned and, when the acting sheriff didn't stop her, walked toward the front door.

"Ms. Keeling, I'd appreciate it if you wouldn't leave the area for a few days. I'd like to talk to you again."

Rowena shot Dylan a smile, then walked out. The acting sheriff didn't try to stop her, but she did watch her go for a few moments. Then she reached into the bag she'd brought, pulled out phone and a stack of what looked like photographs. She turned on the record, gave the date and time and his name and her own and looked up at him.

He was struck again by the intelligence she saw in her eyes. He wondered how many people had underestimated this woman because she was petite and cute as a button, as Rowena had said.

"I already told you that I don't know anyone named Lindsey Martin," he said. "Nor did I get her or anyone else pregnant."

"How about a woman named Athena Grant?" she asked.

He blinked. "Another woman says I've knocked her up?" he demanded.

CAT SLID THE top photograph over to him. It was a copy of the headshot from Athena's passport. As Dylan picked it up, she saw the moment of recognition. "You do know her, don't you, Mr. Walker."

He looked up. His eyes had widened, his jaw had gone slack and some of the color had bled from his face. "I only met her once."

Cat felt her pulse jump. "At the gala you and your wife attended nine months ago?" She knew they had met before that and waited for him to deny it.

He frowned over at her. "No. It was at the wedding."

"Whose wedding?"

"Mine and my wife Ginny's a few weeks earlier. The woman was my sister-in-law Patty's plus one. I'd never met her before."

"You didn't remember her name?"

He shook his head and glanced at the other photographs she'd brought. His eyes widened and shifted from the next photo taken on the morgue table. "She's *dead*?" He sounded shocked. "And the baby?"

"Missing," she said as she watched him put the pieces together.

Dylan leaned back in the chair as if trying to distance himself from all of this.

"It turns out that Athena Grant was more than three weeks overdue," Cat said, recalling what JP had told her. "Which means she didn't get pregnant the night of the gala. Mr. Walker, did you have sex with Athena Grant during your wedding party?"

"No! Are you serious?" he demanded. "I've never heard of anything more…ridiculous. This woman swore to you that I was the father of the baby?" She nodded. "Well, it's not medically possible. Not long after Ginny and I were married, we discovered that I was sterile, something to do with chemicals I came in contact with in my line of work."

"I'm sure that can be proved. Why would Athena Grant tell me her name was Lindsey Martin?"

He shook his head. "I have no idea. I don't recognize either name, and it's not my baby."

She withdrew a form and slid it over to him. "I need you to sign that, authorizing me to take a DNA swab." He was still shaking his head. "I thought you said you weren't the father?"

"I'm not."

"Then there is no reason not to prove it, right?"

He hesitated, but only a moment before he signed the paper and slid it back to her. "Let's get this over with."

Cat met his gaze. Did he think it would be that simple? The deputies returned to say they hadn't found anything in the cottage and were going to the other house and grounds. The moment they were gone, she took the swab and restarted the video recorder. "Tell me about the night of the gala."

His frown formed a deep-set line between his eyes. "I don't understand your interest in the gala, especially if you now think this woman conceived weeks earlier at my wedding."

"Please, Mr. Walker. You were there with your wife. Did you see Athena Grant at the gala?"

"No, I told you. I met her at the wedding. I don't re-member seeing her again after that. I was with my wife all night."

"Except she left the gala without you. Where were you then?"

He sighed. "It was only for a few minutes when Ginny and I got separated. A friend detained me. Other than to get us a drink or go to the men's room, we were together all night. I certainly wasn't away from her long enough to impregnate anyone then or at my wedding."

"Apparently it was a pretty quick seduction."

"Definitely not me then," Dylan said and held her gaze. "I never rush something so important."

Cat felt heat rise to her cheeks. "Why would Athena Grant lie?"

He shook his head. "I have no idea."

"Where were you yesterday evening and night?"

"Here at the ranch. I didn't leave."

"Can anyone corroborate your alibi?" she asked.

He sighed and shook his head. "I was alone. Rowena had left. I don't know what time she got in. Sheriff, the sooner you get that swab to the lab, the sooner you can find out not only who impregnated the woman—but also who killed her and who might have taken the baby. Again, it wasn't me."

"Let's say the baby isn't yours," Cat said. "That doesn't mean you didn't kill her."

Dylan pushed back his chair. "I didn't want to do this,

but I'm not going to answer any more of your questions until my lawyer is present. By then, you should have the DNA results and hopefully have found the missing baby and realized I had nothing to do with any of this."

Chapter Seven

Dylan just wanted everyone to go away. He needed to be alone to think. It felt as if everything was closing in. As he watched the acting sheriff walking up to the big house, he swore. Rowena. What was she still doing here? Certainly, she wasn't here for any reason she'd offered him so far.

In his business, everything had been about careful preparation and timing. Especially timing. That's why it was too much of a coincidence that she happened to be here when Athena Grant had come by the ranch. He didn't believe for a minute that she'd destroyed the note because she couldn't read it and thought the woman was unhinged.

After Ginny's death and what he'd learned about his wife, he'd begun to question everything. Picking up his phone, he searched for Ginny's sister's phone number. Disappointed, but not too surprised, there wasn't a listing. Everyone had gone to cell phones. Still, he searched to see if he could find an address in Denver for Patty Cooper.

When he struck out, he called his friend who'd worked with him on government projects. "I need to know everything you can find out about Ginny Cooper Walker, my late wife, and Patty Cooper, her sister. Last known address, Denver. And Athena Grant and Lindsey Martin, also supposedly out of Denver."

"What specifically are you looking for?"

"I wish I knew. Also…" He wondered why he hadn't thought about this before. "Could you see what you can find on Rowena Keeling. She should still have a DC address."

"Want to tell me what's going on?"

"I would if I knew. Maybe I'm just being paranoid. Or not. Thanks, I appreciate this."

"I'll get back to you as soon as I can. You know if you're in trouble…"

"Not yet. At least not that I know," he said as he watched Acting Sheriff Cat Jameson disappear into his big house, the one Rowena had made herself at home in.

WHEN ROWENA KEELING answered the door, Cat could see just how much the woman had made herself at home. She got the feeling that the woman had checked everything out. There were marks on the rug where something had been dragged and some of the high wood cabinet doors had been left slightly ajar.

Not that she blamed Rowena for wanting to explore the beautiful house. Cat wondered if Dylan's wife, Ginny, had decorated it. If so, she had good taste.

As for Rowena, that she might have designs on Dylan Walker seemed obvious. Even he had had trouble explaining their relationship. Cat had a feeling Rowena wouldn't have that problem.

"I have a few questions," the sheriff said as the woman waved her inside.

"You're really the sheriff?" There was humor in her voice, her expression saying what everyone else was too polite to say. Cat didn't look like she could handle the job—especially pregnant. But she'd been underestimated her entire life. Cat thought in this instance it might actually work in her favor.

"*Acting* sheriff. Why don't we have a seat," Cat suggested since the woman hadn't. "I'll try not to take up too much of your time."

Rowena raised a brow but motioned toward a seating area by the window.

"I'm investigating a murder," Cat said once she'd sat down. Rowena had moved to take a chair closer to the window. She saw at once what the woman had done. The bright sunlight coming through the large windows behind Rowena cast a shadow so Cat wouldn't be able to see her face well—let alone read her expression. It made her wonder if the woman had been interviewed by the law before.

"If you don't mind…" Cat said, motioning to the seat adjacent to her. Rowena pretended not to understand what the problem was but moved nonetheless. "That's much better. I just need you to write down your full name and address and phone number for me." She handed over the notebook and pen and watched the woman scribble it all down before thrusting it back at her.

Flipping to a clean page, she said, "Mr. Walker tells me you're his…?"

A little laugh as she tucked a lock of her blond bob behind her ear and lifted a brow. "Are you asking me what my relationship is with Dylan?"

"Sure, why not? How do you two know each other?"

"I was his wife's best friend. I lived next door. Ginny and I were practically inseparable."

"Oh, so you were at the gala the night she was killed."

Rowena's smile fell. "No, fortunately, otherwise I would have probably been in that car with her."

"With her and Dylan's brother? That's right, you were Ginny's best friend, so she would have confided in you if she was having an affair with Beau Walker."

Rowena waved the question away, pretty much answering it. "I thought you wanted to ask me about that unhinged woman who'd come to the gate."

"Oh, I do, I just need some background. Why weren't you at the gala nine months ago?"

"Shouldn't you be asking me questions about the local murder?" Rowena sighed, then said, "There was a mix-up or something. Ginny felt terrible because she'd paid for my ticket." She glared at the sheriff, fury making her blue eyes bright and brittle.

"When did you arrive here at the ranch?"

"About a week ago."

"Before the woman calling herself Lindsey Martin stopped by the ranch?"

"If you say so."

"Were you at Dylan and Ginny's wedding?" When Cat waited, pen posed over her notebook, Rowena finally said, "No." She hesitated for a moment as if about to lie before she said, "I hadn't met Ginny yet."

"Do you know a woman by the name of Athena Grant?" She saw something in the woman's gaze before Rowena looked away.

"I don't recognize the name. Ginny had a lot of friends."

"This wasn't Ginny's friend. It was her sister Patty's friend that she brought to the wedding."

"What does any of this have to do with the local murder?" the woman demanded impatiently.

"Apparently something since Lindsey Martin lied about her name." Cat pulled out the photos and passed them to her. She saw Rowena's reaction and knew that she was on the right track.

"Her real name was Athena Grant, and she was pregnant with allegedly Dylan Walker's baby and that's why she left the note telling him where she was staying. But Dylan never got that note because you did. And that is why you went to the motel where she was staying and left her the threatening note." Rowena started to protest, but Cat talked over her. "Fortunately, Athena gave me the note and it is now evidence. I suspect your fingerprints are on it, but if not, we can have a handwriting expert compare it with your handwriting."

Rowena seemed to realize that she'd just given the sheriff a sample of her handwriting. Her cheeks flushed, eyes snapping with fury and seemed about ready to argue Cat was wrong.

"You might as well admit it. You are the only one who knew where she was staying. It explains your real reason for not letting Athena in the gate, as well as why you destroyed the note. I'm assuming it has something to do with why you're here on Dylan Walker's ranch as his…houseguest?"

Rowena shot to her feet. "I'm not saying another word without a lawyer."

"I can understand that, but keep in mind, Athena is dead, and the baby is missing. The sooner I find the baby, the better for you since right now you are a suspect in my murder-kidnapping investigation. I could arrest you for threatening the woman only days before she was murdered."

Cat closed her notebook and rose. "What I don't know is if you did it out of jealousy or some other reason you wanted Athena Grant dead and her baby to disappear." Rowena looked as if she could chew nails—or strangle one pregnant acting sheriff. "I'd appreciate it if you hung around the area for a while. But I can always have you picked up if I need to."

DYLAN HAD BEEN watching from the cottage. Not long after the acting sheriff left, Rowena came out of the house, got into her white SUV and took off. Dylan waited until she disappeared into the trees headed for the gate before he grabbed his Stetson and hurried out to his pickup.

He was determined to find out what Rowena was up to. She hadn't just come here to check up on him. Nor was he buying that she had romantic intentions when it came to him. No, something else had brought her to Montana, and he was going to find out what.

When he reached the road, he saw her car in the distance. He'd expected her to go north toward Fortune Creek and Eureka—the same way the sheriff would have gone.

But instead, she was headed south toward the town of Libby. He waited until her car disappeared over a rise in the narrow hilly road before he went after her. He was definitely curious as to where she went every day. How many massages could a woman get? If she was Rowena Keeling, as many as she wanted.

He drove, keeping a good distance between them, which meant that a lot of the time, he couldn't see her ahead of him. It was another beautiful spring day in Montana, not a cloud in the clear robin's-egg blue sky. Snow capped the mountains, glittering in the sunlight. He thought about the mess he was in, but especially the acting sheriff. Did she really suspect him of murder and kidnapping?

As they neared the town of Libby, he turned his thoughts back to Rowena. The town was sprawled next to the Kootenai River, the major river of the Northwest Plateau and one of the uppermost major tributaries of the Columbia River, the largest North American river to empty into the Pacific Ocean.

Not that any of that was why Rowena Keeling had come to town. He'd seen her turn south toward what he guessed was the center of town. Letting a car or two go in front of him, he continued to follow her, all the time hoping this wasn't a wild goose chase.

When she finally pulled over, he did the same a block behind her. He watched her get out of her car and look around before she headed down the sidewalk away from him. Hurrying, he got out and started in her direction. He hadn't done surveillance in years. Had he had time to plan this, he would have at least changed his clothing.

But Rowena didn't look back before turning into a doorway along the main drag. He waited a couple of doors down. If she'd spotted the tail, she might have just stepped into the store to see if he hurried to catch up to her. After a few minutes, he decided that she hadn't spotted him and walked closer to the business where she'd gone inside.

Swearing, he saw that it was a massage studio and hair salon. Turning back to his pickup, he debated how long to hang out. His impulsive decision to follow her felt foolish and a complete waste of time. But time was something he had a lot of these days. He climbed behind the wheel to wait. Massages could take an hour or more. Or at least Ginny's had taken that long. Then again, for all he knew, she'd used them as an excuse to meet someone. His brother?

He shoved that thought away and realized he was thirsty. He should have at least brought something to eat and drink if this was going to take—

Rowena came out of the studio, looked both ways, then walked quickly back to her car. He started his pickup. She hadn't had time for a haircut or a massage. So why drive all the way down here when whatever she'd done probably could have been handled with a phone call?

He hadn't gone far when Rowena turned off the main drag, went a block and turned again. She was making it harder to follow her, but he wasn't about to lose her. She turned left again, taking her back to the main highway.

By the time he saw her again, she was turning north toward the ranch. He followed for a little way, seeing her car in the distance, then turned off and went back to Libby. He had no idea what he was going to do at the studio salon, just that he couldn't leave yet.

After parking, he walked down the block and pushed open the door. He was instantly hit with the sweet scent of pampered women. Moving to the reception desk, he said, "I'd like to get a package for my wife's birthday. The whole ballgame. What would you suggest?"

The just-out-of-high-school-looking girl behind the

counter smiled and pulled out a brochure. "What of these do you think she would like?"

He glanced down the list, thinking of Cat. "She's seven months pregnant."

"We have someone who does pregnancy massages. Also, she might like this." She pointed to a body moisturizer wrap.

"This is more difficult than I thought it would be," he said glancing at the hair salon along one side of the building. Several women were getting haircuts, chatting with the stylists. "My wife's friend was just in here. Rowena Keeling? If you can tell me what she gets done."

The young woman hesitated for a moment. "Let me check."

He spelled the name. She leafed through the reservations book but found that Rowena Keeling had never had a massage or hair appointment. "That's odd," he said frowning. "I just saw her coming out of here." He described her.

"Oh, her," the receptionist said. "I believe she just went back to talk to one of the massage therapists."

"Oh, which one was that?" he asked, trying to be as nonchalant as possible.

"Sharese." He waited for a last name but saw one wasn't coming.

"Thank you. Clearly, I need to give this more thought." He took the brochure and walked out. Back in his pickup, he looked on the brochure. Just as he expected, Sharese's last name was listed. Sharese Harmon.

Dylan smiled to himself. It hadn't been a wasted trip after all.

Chapter Eight

Cat had a lot of time to think on her way back to her office in Fortune Creek. Her thoughts kept circling back to Dylan Walker. Did she just want to believe him because he seemed so sincere? Or was she being taken in by his extremely good innocent act? She'd never let a handsome man unnerve her, yet the pain she saw in him did make her feel compassion for him. It hadn't been all that long ago that he'd lost his wife and now this. Whatever this was.

All Cat knew was that she had a dead woman and missing baby mystery to solve. She didn't feel like she was getting anywhere with this case. Yesterday, she'd made dozens of calls to hospitals, motels, hotels, bed and breakfasts. No woman matching Athena's description had checked in. As pregnant as Athena was, she would have stood out.

Cat found Helen knitting. "Any messages?"

The older woman shook her head without looking up from whatever she was making. It wasn't until Cat was sitting in her office that she noticed how small the knitting project appeared to be. What startled her most was that the yarn was blue.

She opened her door and approached the receptionist-dispatcher-knitter. "Are you making this by any chance for the missing baby?"

"What if I am?" Helen said without missing a stitch.

"I think that's nice, but what makes you think the infant is a boy?" Cat had only recently learned that the baby was male.

"I saw the way she was carrying. Low. Knew it was going to be a boy."

"Huh," Cat said.

"Just like you're carrying high. Girl."

She didn't comment on that, but she hadn't told anyone that she was having a girl. Nor did she feel any compulsion to admit that Helen was right. She was more interested in where Helen got her information. "What else do you know about the woman?"

"She was lying."

"Based on what?"

"Years of experience in this office," the older woman said with authority.

So maybe she hadn't been listening in on phone calls from the coroner. "All right, then who's the father of the baby?"

"That's the million-dollar question, isn't it." She reached over as a call came in, picked up her old-fashioned headset and answered, "Fortune Creek Sheriff's Department. Yep, she's right here. It's for you," she said as she put the call through to Cat's desk and went back to knitting.

Helen was making baby clothing for the missing infant. Maybe it was the pregnancy hormones, but she liked this side of Helen.

In her office, she took the call. It was the coroner

asking if she'd gotten his report. She'd just dropped off Dylan Walker's DNA sample, too early to have results. She tapped her computer to life and saw that JP had sent her the autopsy results. The weapon used to kill her had been a .38 caliber. Three shots to the heart at close range. Why would Athena Grant have let the man who threatened her get that close? Unless he forced his way in to wherever she'd been staying.

Nothing made sense. Why hadn't the woman stayed at the hotel across the street? She might still be alive and her baby... Where was her baby? Was he still alive?

She turned her attention to what JP was saying. "Wait, what?"

"She had help delivering the baby."

"But the hospitals and emergency rooms—"

"Not at the hospital. That alarm you put out about the missing baby got a response. I know the woman who owns the motel. She called me."

"The baby's been found?"

"No, but a motel maid called to say she thought a woman had given birth in one of her rooms she cleaned. Bloody bedsheets and the placenta in the trash. The man in the next unit hearing a baby cry in the middle of the night." He gave her the name of the motel, The Siesta Vista, and told her to talk to the owner.

The moment she disconnected, she found what photos she could of anyone who might have helped Athena that could have been connected. The list was short: Ginny Cooper Walker (dead), Patty Cooper Harper, Ginny's sister, and Rowena Keeling, a complete stranger according to her. She got mugshots from drivers' licenses or in the case of Patty Cooper Harper, her school ID.

If it hadn't been either Patty or Rowena having helped Athena have her baby, then Cat was out of suspects.

BACK AT THE RANCH, Dylan noted Rowena's car was in front of the house. As soon as he'd returned to where he had internet service, he'd made the call to a contact he could trust. The conversation though now had him feeling as if he'd fallen in a rabbit hole.

"Are you aware that all of the women you asked me about were adopted?"

"Why is that important?" Dylan had asked.

"Russia formalized its international adoption program in the middle of 1991," his government contact had told him. "That year only twelve children were adopted by American families. That number topped a thousand by 1994."

"Wait, you're telling me that Ginny, her sister Patty and Athena Grant were all born in Russia and adopted by American families?" Dylan had said.

"All adopted the same year by families in the Denver area," his friend had told him. "Ginny and Patty to the same family, the Coopers. Athena Grant to Lindsey and Lloyd Martin."

He let out a curse. Now at least he knew where Athena had gotten the name she'd used the day she'd come out to the ranch. Because she thought he would recognize it? He frowned and felt a start. Had Rowena recognized it?

"What about Rowena Keeling and Sharese Harmon?" he asked, waiting for confirmation as he looked toward the big house and saw Rowena headed his way. He wasn't surprised that she would come down to see him. She'd be curious to know what he'd told the sheriff and deputies earlier.

"Keeling and Harmon were in a later batch of Russian babies adopted to American families that same year, along with Harmon's brother Luca. You had no idea your wife was adopted?"

"Not a clue. But there was a lot about Ginny I didn't know, as it turns out. Wait, Sharese has a brother named Luca who was also adopted. By the same family? Where?"

"By Bob and Lynette Harmon of Missoula, Montana."

"Whoa, that close by," Dylan had said, unsure what to make of the information, but knowing that it had to be the connection he'd been looking for.

"I'm curious why you would be asking about these people."

He hesitated to even voice it. "Is it possible they are part of a sleeper cell?" He knew from his career that there had been instances of real-life "sleeper agents" who'd dealt in spying, espionage, sedition, treason and even...assassinations on behalf of their mother country leaders.

"It's possible, I suppose. All from the same area. If they all knew they were adopted from Russia, became friends, were approached by someone, I suppose that's what they might have become."

"I'm worried that's exactly what happened," he admitted.

"What do you plan to do with this information?"

"Don't worry, I won't tell anyone where I got it."

"But maybe you should tell someone about what you've discovered," his friend said. "Someone who can stop whatever this group might be up to."

"At this point, I have no evidence. Once I do...
Thanks for this information. I owe you." He disconnected, unable to shake off the feeling that he was on to something. He remembered some of the questions his wife had asked him about his job. He'd assumed she only knew about the real one—not the undercover one. But now he wondered if it was why she'd married him.

She'd definitely been the one to pursue him, he thought looking back. It had been more than flattering. She'd literally swept him off his feet with her enthusiasm for all things, especially him. What a fool he'd been, he thought with a curse.

What scared him was where his brother might have come into all of this—if he had. Beau had always colored outside the lines. His job, like Dylan's, had put him in places and situations that were dangerous in so many ways. Had Beau gotten involved with the wrong people? The wrong people being Ginny Cooper Walker? Is that why the two of them were targeted?

He thought about the acquaintance who'd detained him the night of the gala. The man had saved his life. Was that what he'd intended to do? Now he was suspicious of everyone and everything that had happened.

Raking a hand through his hair, Dylan felt his mind spinning. What if nothing was as it seemed? And more to the point, what if Rowena Keeling had been in on all of it? That would certainly explain how she'd gotten into their lives and why Ginny had let her.

But right now, he didn't have the time to consider what to even do about it. Groaning, he saw Rowena climb his deck steps.

The acting sheriff—he couldn't help thinking of her

as Cat from the first time she'd introduced herself—had asked his houseguest not to leave the area. Which gave Rowena the perfect excuse for hanging around longer. Not that he couldn't kick her out. But wasn't he smarter to keep her close?

Athena Grant was dead. The acting sheriff seemed to think not only had he fathered the woman's child, but also that he'd killed her and done what with the baby? He felt sick at the thought of the infant. He had wanted a child so badly with Ginny.

As Rowena reached the deck, he walked out to her. As he did, he tried to gauge how her interview had gone with the sheriff earlier. He really doubted Cat would have been intimidated by Rowena in the least. "Have a nice talk with the sheriff? You left pretty quickly afterward."

She mugged a face. "I had an appointment. Do you even have to ask how it went with the *acting* sheriff?" She sounded cocky, but when she moved to the edge of the deck and took hold of the railing, he thought she looked…nervous? Or was it scared?

Until that moment, he hadn't even suspected that she might have done something to Athena Grant and her baby. But it had been Rowena who'd turned the woman away at the gate, who had gone down to the mailbox to take the note. He swore under his breath as he moved to her, touching her arm, forcing her to look at him.

"Tell me you had nothing to do with that woman's death or her missing baby."

She stared at him as if shocked that he would ask such a thing. "You can't be serious. Who do you think I am?" she demanded indignantly, but she didn't quite pull it off.

"That's just it, I have no idea."

Her expression changed quickly to coy, which he assumed was her default. "Because you haven't wanted to get to know me, your loss." She cocked her head at him, her blue eyes alight with mischief. "What did you tell your cute acting sheriff about me?" she asked coquettishly. "I'm curious how you described our...relationship."

"We don't have one, and quite frankly, I'm not even sure how to describe you, let alone explain what you're doing here," he said.

"You shouldn't have to explain yourself to some small-town sheriff. *Really.*" Rowena could get more meaning into a single word. "Who does she think she is to question you—let alone me, your houseguest?"

His houseguest. It hadn't slipped his mind that Rowena had arrived shortly before all this had begun. He couldn't imagine how she might have orchestrated it, though. But then again, there was a good chance that she'd lied about having never met Athena Grant. He had no proof that the women had all known each other, but he'd bet his life on it. The thought unsettled him as he realized he just might be doing exactly that.

He frowned, trying to remember if Rowena had been at the wedding. No, Ginny allegedly hadn't met her yet because Rowena hadn't moved in next door. But that didn't mean the two of them didn't know each other *before* Rowena moved into their building. How could he forget that everything Ginny had told him probably was a lie? But did that include her relationship with Rowena—and Athena Grant? He now knew that all four of them were connected by birth in Russia. All four adopted by American families in Denver. And now there were two more, Sharese and Luca Harmon, adopted in Missoula—not all that far away.

He shook his aching head, afraid it was starting to make sense. Rowena had paid a visit to Sharese, he had to assume she too was in on whatever they were up to. His wife's supposed best friend being here now wasn't a coincidence.

Still he wasn't sure how all the pieces fit together. Athena Grant had been pregnant, that much was true. For some reason she'd tried to contact him with this bogus claim that he was the father of her baby. She even went to the sheriff to get him to talk to her. Why go to all that trouble? Because she was trying to warn him?

Dylan hated to think she'd done it so she could get to him without the others suspecting her true reason. Maybe she'd wanted to tell him about Ginny and his brother. Or warn him that they were coming for him next? If he hadn't gotten stopped on the way out of the gala, he and his brother and wife would have been killed. But if Ginny and Beau were working for Russia, why kill them? His head whirled with too many possibilities.

"Are you all right?" Rowena asked, frowning at him. He realized he'd been rubbing his temples, his head aching. "I could use a drink. Why don't I make one for you too?"

Earlier he'd wanted Rowena to leave. Now though he realized that nothing was quite like he'd thought. No way was he going to let this woman make him a drink. He'd never mistrusted her more than he did right now.

But he also needed to now what was going on. "Maybe it's time you tell me who Rowena Keeling really is."

Chapter Nine

The motel was a former motor inn on the edge of Eureka, U-shaped with scalloped gingerbread trim over the windows and a general look of neglect. Cat entered the office, a bell dinging overhead as she did. The smell of cooked cabbage was almost enough to bring back her morning sickness.

An older woman appeared looking harried as she wiped her hands on her apron. The sign on the registration desk said Karla Brooks, owner. "Only have one double left. Seventy-five dollars. Just one night?" She looked up for the first time and noticed the uniform. Disappointment made her face seem to sag.

"I'm Acting Sheriff Cat Jameson from Fortune Creek. I'd like to ask you a few questions about the woman who gave birth in one of your units."

Sighing, she said, "Could we make this quick. I'm in the middle of making dinner."

"No problem. Did you check her in?" A nod. "Did you get her name?" The woman opened her book and turned it so Cat could see the name Lindsey Martin. "She pay cash?" Another nod. "Was the woman alone?"

"Far as I know."

"Did she seem to be in distress? In pain?" A shrug. "Did she make any request other than a room?"

"Wanted the one at the end."

"Is that the one you gave her?" A nod. "Did you see anyone else with her before she left?"

"Nope."

"I'm asking because the baby she gave birth to is missing and the woman was murdered."

The motel manager swallowed, her eyes misting over. "She was the one?"

"It would appear so. If you saw something, anything at all, it might help us find her killer and—"

"That's the missing baby boy?" Her voice broke. "I have a son." She looked away for a moment before she turned back to Cat. "The next morning, the man in the adjacent room did come by to complain about not being able to get any sleep. Said there were people coming and going. He heard a car pull up, door slam and someone enter that room in the middle of the night. He couldn't get back to sleep because of the moaning." She lifted a brow as if it was obvious what he thought that was about. "Then he said he heard a baby cry. Sometime later he was relieved to hear the person leave and drive away so he could get some sleep."

"He didn't hear the baby cry again?" A head shake. "I'm going to need his name," Cat said. "But this has been really helpful." She thought about asking to see the room but knew there would be nothing to see after all this time.

Outside in the parking lot, she made the call from her patrol SUV. She couldn't help thinking about Athena in labor, giving birth in a motel room instead of a hospital, someone helping her. The same someone who took the baby?

The man who'd been in the adjacent motel room told her pretty much the same thing the motel owner had. "Do you remember anything else that could help? The sound of the car engine? Perhaps you heard a voice."

"Two females," he said. "Not sure how I know that, just that I do. Also on the car… Sorry, they all sound alike now. There is one thing. The one who left, she opened the car door, but took a few minutes before I heard the engine start up. I think she put the baby in some kind of car seat."

"You didn't look out the window?" She heard him hesitate.

"I did look." He sighed. "I didn't get a good look at the woman, but she definitely had the baby."

Cat pried a description of the woman out of him. He'd gotten a better look than he'd thought. He described Patty Cooper Harper.

She hurriedly called the DCI, Montana Division of Criminal Investigations, and asked for their help in locating Ginny's sister, Patty Cooper Harper.

According to the description the man in the motel room next to Athena's had given Cat, Patty had helped deliver the baby. That meant she had to have known the baby was coming and had been prepared with whatever she needed, including a car seat. That gave Cat hope that the infant was safe and being cared for.

It was dark by the time she headed back to Fortune Creek. She drove along the narrow road, trees etched dark against the fading light of day. The cool spring night, as pretty as it was, made her melancholy. She hadn't let herself think about the future—or the past, determined to live day by day and think only of her daughter growing inside her. Tonight, though, the past came creeping in, bringing tears of pain and sorrow.

Her cell phone rang as she neared Fortune Creek. She hurriedly wiped her tears and picked up.

"This case just keeps getting more interesting," JP said the moment she answered. "Did you know that male cells have been found in maternal blood even decades after a pregnancy?"

"I did not," Cat said, darkness dropping like a cloak over the road ahead. Her headlights cut a swatch of light through the trees standing like sentinels on both sides. "But if you're trying to tell me that you obtained the father of the baby's DNA from the deceased woman's blood—"

"I am."

That stopped her. "I thought we'd have to wait until we found the baby," she said. "You know who fathered Athena Grant's baby?"

"The crime lab just called to tell me that they found a match. Are you sitting down?"

"I am." She braced herself, thinking of how absolutely sure Dylan Walker was that he hadn't fathered Athena Grant's baby. "Is the baby Dylan's?"

"Looked that way at first. Definitely a relative. Does he happen to have a brother?"

"He did. Beau Walker. But he died nine months ago."

"Like I said, interesting case. It appears that Beau is the father of the missing baby, unless there is another brother."

"Nope. Looks like I'm going back out to the ranch

tomorrow," she said as she saw the lights of Fortune Creek ahead and felt a strange sense of relief. Something about the night was getting to her, making her feel anxious, making her feel afraid. She was tired from being on her feet all day and hungry. Once in her apartment, she planned to make herself some canned tomato soup and a grilled cheese for dinner.

As she pulled into the tiny, isolated Montana town, she saw Rowena's vehicle was parked up the street. Movement caught her attention. A woman and man arguing in the shadows on the side of the Fortune Creek Hotel across from the sheriff's office. She probably wouldn't have noticed them except that a car went past, its headlights bathed the two in light for a moment. They'd both looked in her direction as if surprised to see a car going by.

She recognized the woman first. Rowena Keeling. The man was one of the two she'd seen going into the hotel whatever day that had been. She was losing track, each day slipping away so fast, and the baby still not found.

Parking behind the sheriff's department building, she made the hike to the second floor over her office. As she did, she speculated on what the two had been arguing about. Clearly, they knew each other. She'd gotten the impression that the only reason Rowena had come to Montana was to see Dylan Walker.

Once in her apartment, she didn't turn on the lights. Instead, she moved to the front window to look out, curious if the two were still out there in the dark. But the spot where they had been was now empty, just like the main street of town. Nor was the vehicle she recognized as Rowena Keeling's still parked down the street in front of the café any longer.

As Cat turned on a lamp and closed the curtains, she made a mental note to ask a few more questions when she saw the woman at Dylan's ranch in the morning.

Unfortunately, things didn't go as she had planned, though. The next morning, she was awakened by the two men she'd seen going into the hotel. They'd flashed their FBI IDs, demanding the file on Athena Grant.

"I'M GOING TO be honest with you, Dylan," his lawyer said. "I don't like them reopening the bombing case. It was never really closed, but all I can think is that they have new evidence. I have to warn you, I have been contacted by the prosecutor's office. They wanted your address in Montana and a phone number. Said they were updating their contact sheet."

He swore under his breath. "Right. You have no idea what might really be going on?"

"No, since they haven't filed any charges against anyone. But if they suspect that your wife and brother were having an affair…they might get the idea that you had something to do with the bombing. Your experience in the service, as well as with your job, puts you in the category of explosives expert."

Dylan didn't need his lawyer to tell him that. "You think someone is trying to frame me?"

"You liquidating everything you owned and moving to Montana does look suspicious."

"Anything I do right now makes me look suspicious," he said, thinking of the trouble that had followed him out here to Montana. Ginny's sister's friend was dead, her baby missing. Did it matter that it wasn't his baby? It would still raise suspicion. The timing couldn't be worse, but maybe that too wasn't a coincidence.

He ended the call and tossed down his phone. No one seemed to know exactly why the investigation into his wife's and brother's deaths was being reopened. But Rowena had been right at least about that. Was she also right about there being some discrepancy with identifying the remains? Or was his lawyer closer to the truth and they were coming after the jealous husband.

Rowena had stopped by early this morning. She'd mentioned a massage appointment in Eureka and had left. He thought this time she might be telling the truth and didn't follow her. Instead, he called an old friend for surveillance equipment, saying he needed to do some tracking. He planned to put it on her car if he got the chance.

Now, standing out on his deck, he ran a hand through his long hair, wondering idly when he'd last gotten it cut. Not that it mattered—at least to him. He had more important things to worry about. The last thing he wanted to think about was Ginny and her death. He could still see her in his mind's eye quickly getting into the town car that pulled up to the curb and it quickly driving away—only to stop up the street. As he'd stepped into the street, planning to try to catch her, it had blown up. He had tried to recall his mindset at that moment. He'd known something was going on with his wife that night. She hadn't been herself. That she would get into a car and take off like that—

At the time he hadn't known who was driving. That came later. He hadn't even known his brother was back in the states. Why had Beau been picking up Ginny? He didn't know, probably never would. Or why she'd seemed to be in such a hurry. At the gala, she'd been by his side on her phone when he'd been stopped on the way out. When he looked again, Ginny was heading for the door. He had excused himself and tried to catch up to her. Hadn't he known then that something was up? That she'd been acting oddly all night? He'd gotten the feeling that there was something she wanted to tell him.

He thought about how upset she'd been when they'd discovered he couldn't father a baby. They'd actually talked about adopting. What a fool he'd been, since after her death, he'd found the birth control pills she'd been faithfully taking in her side of the bathroom cabinet. Ginny had never wanted to have a child with him—or anyone else apparently.

What he would never understand is what his brother had to do with any of it. He assumed Beau and Ginny had been having an affair. He'd found evidence of the two of them meeting at hotels and bars before the day they died. If he had been able to find that evidence, he didn't doubt the investigators looking into the bombing could find it as well.

But what if it hadn't been an affair? What if Beau had gotten involved in something even more dangerous and now the feds had discovered it? Dylan just hoped that the two of them hadn't made it appear that he was part of it.

The gate intercom buzzed, making him start. He moved to it and his heart fell. The acting sheriff was back.

"Need to see you," she said.

He didn't even ask, he just buzzed her in.

Chapter Ten

Dylan was standing on his deck as Cat drove up—in the same spot where she'd first seen him. Only then, she'd thought he might be the ranch caretaker. Today he was dressed much as he had been that day. Jeans, boots, a flannel shirt. Except today, he wore a Stetson over his dark hair.

Under the brim of his hat, he looked just as grim as he had the first day she'd met him. Maybe even grimmer as if now expecting bad news. She glanced toward the cottage and then up to the big house. She didn't see Rowena's car and, while relieved that she wasn't here since she wanted to talk to Dylan alone, Cat hoped she hadn't taken off. She now knew the woman was up to more than just trying to lasso herself a rich rancher.

"Rowena's not here," Dylan said as if reading her mind. "But she hasn't left for good." He didn't sound happy about that. "Come on in. Can I offer you some coffee? Decaf if you'd like. I have tea too."

The FBI agents had grilled her all morning and part of the afternoon about the case. She figured they were going to tell her to step aside and let them take over. To her surprise, they didn't. Apparently, they needed her since they were after who had given the order for Athena to be killed—not the killer.

Were they willing to tell her what all this was about? No. "But you're willing for me to risk my life and my baby's not knowing who I can trust?" she'd demanded.

"Isn't that your job?" one of the agents asked.

She'd smiled. "Yes. What about Dylan Walker?"

"We're not interested in him," one of the agents said.

She'd been relieved to hear them say that. Her instincts about him had been right. She needed to keep trusting herself. But that also meant trusting Dylan Walker. So, it was late afternoon by the time she'd driven out to the ranch.

"Decaf would be fine," she said, smiling her thanks and following him into the kitchen. She noticed that his hair was still damp from a shower. She caught the fresh scent of him and couldn't blame Rowena for having designs on the man—if that's what at least some of this was.

Dylan poured them both a mug of coffee, then offered her a seat at the table. She sat, cupping the mug in her hands. Her daughter had been kicking up a storm all morning.

"I know you didn't come here to tell me that my DNA matches," he said. "I can also tell that the baby hasn't been found so there's still hope."

She smiled in surprise. "I didn't know you were psychic."

"I'm usually not good at reading people, terrible at it, but you…" He shrugged. "You've got news though, but it's not horrible news. Am I right?"

"We have a DNA match. Athena Grant was pregnant with your brother's child."

Dylan put down his mug, sloshing the coffee onto the table—not that he noticed. "What?"

"Unless you have another brother with similar DNA…"

He shook his head. *"Beau?"* He scrubbed his hands over his face. He looked up. "I don't understand."

"From what the coroner said, she probably conceived at your wedding. I'm assuming your brother—"

"Was my best man."

She could see how hard this was on him. "Were you and your brother close?"

"I thought so. But then he died with my wife the night of the gala." He met her gaze. "I'm sure you know all about that. I didn't even know he was back in the states. Usually, he called. I have no idea why he picked up Ginny that night. I saw her on her phone and then she left…" He sighed. "After they both died, I just assumed he was having an affair with her. Everyone assumed that." Dylan looked at her hopefully. "Did Athena say she and Beau were together?"

"She said it happened only once, but that doesn't mean it was true. She lied about everything else. Was Athena maid of honor or maybe a bridesmaid?"

"No, Ginny's sister Patty was her matron of honor. It was a small wedding, just friends and family. A short engagement." He seemed to realize she would wonder why the rush. "We jumped into marriage after knowing each other for just a few months. Ginny…" Shaking his head, he continued, "I thought I knew her. I didn't. I wasn't thinking clearly. It all happened too fast and for the wrong reasons." He let out a bitter laugh. "I wanted what she was offering me, settling down, having a home, kids, that whole happy ever after. Turns out I couldn't have made her pregnant even if she wasn't lying and taking birth control pills."

He stopped speaking as if wishing he hadn't said so much and put his head in his hands for a few moments. "This missing baby…"

"Your nephew."

Dylan looked up and swore. "I'm sorry, it hasn't sunk in yet. This is such a shock. It makes me question everything. You still don't know what she did with the infant?" Cat shook her head. "But why would this woman tell you her name was Lindsey Martin, and I was the father of her baby?"

"Maybe she thought that was the only way she could get to see you."

He stared at her for a moment before raking his hand through his hair. "I think you might be right. Otherwise, it makes no sense. You think there was something she wanted to tell me, and she was using the baby as a way to force me to see her? But wouldn't she just leave it in a note?"

"Maybe she did," Cat said, making him curse.

"And my houseguest destroyed it."

"Yes—after Rowena went to Athena's motel room and left a threatening note that was allegedly from you."

"*What?* Rowena admitted that to you?" he demanded, shooting to his feet to pace the room.

"Apparently she has designs on you," Cat said. "And saw Athena as a threat to her plan."

He stopped pacing to look at her, putting her instincts on alert. He knew something and he was debating telling her. After a moment, he said, "This isn't about Rowena having romantic designs on me. I'm afraid it's more cunning and dangerous."

DYLAN SIGHED AS he considered what he was about to do. "I need to be honest with you." He sat back down near her. He'd survived at his job by trusting his gut. He was going to do the same right now. "Rowena isn't here to seduce me."

"No?"

"No. It's complicated." He rubbed the back of his neck.

"I know you're trying to decide if you can trust me. I would have felt the same way."

"But you don't now?"

"Two agents from the FBI stopped by to see me this morning." Her gaze was intent on him. "They were very interested in Athena Grant, but not you. Tell me about your job overseas."

Dylan looked into her eyes, unable to look away even if he'd wanted to. "You know I can't, but still you're wondering if you can trust me. Yet the FBI doesn't suspect me, right? You wouldn't be here unless they already answered your question. Unfortunately, the bombing and now whatever is going on threatens to expose me and others I worked with."

"Does it involve Athena Grant? If you know something about her death, I need you to tell me. I know you want to trust me. You can. Just be honest with me."

He smiled and nodded. "I didn't know anything, until this morning," he said and proceeded to repeat what his friend had found out about Ginny, Athena, Patty and

Rowena. "Lindsey Martin was the name of the mother who adopted Athena."

"That would explain why she used that name. Did she think you would recognize it?"

"Maybe. She could have thought that Ginny had told me her mother's name. She hadn't. But all I can think is what are the chances they all four didn't know they were adopted from Russia?"

She hugged herself as if feeling the same chill he had at the news. He wondered for a moment if he'd made a mistake by telling her. He told himself he didn't know this woman. Trusting her could be a mistake. Yet, he didn't believe that. Still, it was risky. But the acting sheriff was already in danger the moment she got the Athena Grant case.

Cat seemed to digest what he'd told her before she said, "You think the four are part of a sleeper cell?"

"I do," he admitted, glad he could say it out loud. "I followed Rowena to Libby where she met with someone named Sharese Harmon. Turns out that Sharese and her brother Luca were also both born in Russia and adopted by a family in Missoula."

Cat was shaking her head. "You think they are all involved?" He nodded. "But why kill Athena?"

"Why kill Ginny and my brother?" he asked with a shake of his head.

"I probably shouldn't be sharing this with you, but the two FBI agents who came by my office this morning demanded everything I had on Athena Grant's death."

"I knew it." He swore, looking relieved. "So, we are on to something. It could be why I've heard that they are looking into the bombing again. What a damned fool I was for marrying a woman with this kind of secret."

"She never told you she was adopted?" He shook his head. "You think it's all tied together, the bombing, what's happening now?"

"I bought this ranch before the wedding, but after the bombing and what I learned about my wife and brother, I moved out here because I wanted to be alone. I was convinced my cover was blown. But then nothing happened." He shook his head. "But I should have known the moment Rowena showed up here. I was certainly suspicious about her motives, but then when all the rest of this began to happen…"

"As I said earlier, I think Athena was trying to tell you something," Cat said. "Which could explain why Rowena destroyed her note telling you where she would be—and then went to the motel to threaten her, leaving her a note when she didn't find her. She was warning her to stay away from you and not tell you whatever it was she really wanted you to know. Obviously, Rowena knew Athena wasn't pregnant with your child, but maybe she wanted you to know about your brother's baby, don't you think? By the time she came to me, she must have known they would kill her. I'm sure she was worried about what would happen to her infant."

He nodded. "I think you're right. She wanted me to know what was going on, but also about my nephew and maybe how my brother was involved." Getting to his feet, he said, "I could use a drink. Can I get you a sparkling water?"

She nodded and followed him into the living room. As he poured Bourbon into a rocks glass, he spoke as if running it all through his mind. "I never could understand what Ginny saw in Rowena. Once she moved next door to us, she was at our house all the time. It felt... off. I got the feeling that Ginny didn't like her, and I certainly didn't. But it wasn't like Ginny not to get her out of her life if that was the case. She'd dropped others who'd tried to hang on to her in a heartbeat."

He brought his drink and her sparkling water over and motioned that they should sit in the living room where it was more comfortable.

"Where do you think your brother fits in?"

"I have no idea. Knowing my brother, he could have been working with them. Maybe he only slept with Athena one time. Or maybe they were lovers and they were working together. But why kill him?" He took a sip of his drink.

Cat thought for a moment. "If Ginny wanted out, is there a reason she would have asked your brother for help?"

He felt his flesh rise in goose bumps. "Instead of me?" He shook his head. "Athena and Ginny must have dragged him into something. I can't imagine what help Beau would have been. Then again, I'd lost track of what he'd been doing while abroad. Who knows what he might have gotten into. Knowing my brother, he might have thought he could handle it and that got him killed."

CAT HAD A moment to wonder what she was doing. Dylan had opened up to her. She'd told him about the FBI. They'd both revealed probably more than they should have since she was the law and not long ago he'd been a suspect. But he was also a man with a past, one apparently he needed to keep hidden.

We all have our secrets, she thought as she looked at him. The question was, did she trust him? *With your life?* She'd better because she was gambling on it by opening up to him.

"This changes things," she said, realizing it was true.

"Look, I understand, Cat—sorry, I meant to say Sheriff. I've been worried that I involved you and your baby in my mess and it's dangerous."

She shook her head. "It's my job. But please, I think after this we could call each other by our first names— at least when we're alone."

"That would be nice. We've wandered into questionable territory. My fault. I just thought you should know what I found out, what we might be dealing with."

What *we* might be dealing with. He was right. They were both involved in this. It made sense to help each other since she couldn't shake the feeling that if this was what they suspected, they were both at risk. Also, she would bet that Dylan might have more expertise in this area than she did.

The two FBI agents had said they would be in touch and had driven away, so she couldn't count on them. All she knew was that at least one of them had met with Rowena. Maybe Dylan had some thoughts about that after what he'd discovered today.

Taking a breath, she said, "I saw one of the FBI agents in the alleyway by the hotel in town the other night with Rowena. They appeared to be arguing."

"You think Rowena is working with them? Or at least pretending to?"

Cat shrugged. "Yesterday I found out that someone helped birth the baby. We know that Athena nursed the infant, then it appears whoever helped her left, possibly with the infant since the man in the next room didn't hear the baby cry again. What might have happened after that, we don't know. In the wee hours of the morning, Athena was shot, killed and dumped along the road near Fortune Creek—just miles from the sheriff's department."

"You're thinking Rowena?" He shook his head. "I can't imagine her delivering a baby in my wildest dreams. But there is one person my friend hasn't been able to locate. Patty Cooper, Ginny's sister."

"I thought of that, too. I'm hoping if true, she has the baby and won't let anything happen to him." She told Dylan what the man at the motel had told her about the person's description fitting Patty and that the person possibly had a car seat for the baby.

Dylan swore. "If only I'd been here the morning Athena stopped by to see me," he said.

"I doubt it would have saved her since Rowena would have found out either way." He nodded and took another drink. She opened her water. "If she is working with the feds, then why not let Athena talk to you?"

"Like I said, she could be a double agent. I wouldn't put anything past that woman," Dylan said.

"What are you going to do about her?" Cat asked.

"My first instinct is to throw her out. But if I want answers, then I need to let her think I'm not on to her."

DYLAN REALIZED THAT she hadn't seemed to have heard him. "Cat?" He liked the sound of her name on his lips. He liked her, and that scared him. He'd liked her from the first time he met her—when she'd come out to accuse him of all kinds of things. He thought about the last woman he fell for quickly and told himself to slow down.

Cat seemed to understand what they might be digging into, but he couldn't stand the thought of anything happening to her or her baby. They already had one mother dead, her baby missing.

"I thought you'd bought the ranch after your wife was killed," she said, looking lost in thought.

"No, months before the wedding."

"Your wife knew about the ranch?"

"I'm not sure what you're getting at, but yes, it was kind of a wedding present to us both, a new beginning." He could see where it could be misconstrued, though, that he had been planning to kill his wife and her lover, but he didn't think that was what Cat was getting at.

"The two of you came out here to see it?" she asked.

He started to say yes but remembered. "Ginny came out earlier to furnish the big house. I came out later." He frowned. "What are you thinking?"

"Have you been over to the house since you've been back this time? Especially since Rowena has been staying there?"

"No, why?"

"When I went over there to ask her a few questions, I noticed something that at the time didn't seem odd but does now. It looked as if an object had been dragged out from the wall in the living room. It left a mark on the carpet. Also the doors on several of the high cabinets in the hallway had been left slightly ajar." She met his gaze. "Now I'm wondering if Rowena had gone through the place maybe—"

"Looking for something?"

"Had you ever planned to live in the big house?" she asked.

"With Ginny…" he said, "since I thought we both wanted a lot of children." He felt his eyes widen. "You think Ginny left something over there knowing I wouldn't look for it—let alone find it if anything happened to her."

Cat touched the end of her nose and grinned at him. "Think there's time to check it out before Rowena returns?"

"Let's go."

Chapter Eleven

Cat had no idea what they were looking for. But maybe Rowena hadn't either. The house was enormous. She could see why Dylan hadn't wanted to stay here—even with his wife—until they had children to fill it. She wondered how Ginny had felt about that.

Once inside, he said, "Shall we start on the upper level and work our way down?" He pointed to a wooden panel that magically opened as he touched it, exposing a small elevator. "Ladies first."

She smiled and stepped into the confined space, which normally wouldn't have bothered her. But when Dylan entered, it suddenly felt even smaller. He was average height and weight, but in the elevator, he seemed a whole lot larger. She found herself very aware of him and his enticing male scent.

Keep this professional, she thought and almost laughed. *Call me Cat.* They were way past professional. She'd told him things she had no business telling him—but he'd done the same. He however wasn't the law, she was. Yet, they wouldn't be here in this house looking for clues if they both hadn't shared what they knew. Didn't that make her a good investigator?

She didn't kid herself as the elevator door opened and she quickly escaped. The scent of him followed her, as did the memory of his flat stomach, the muscles of his arms, the way his jeans fit in the back. She felt herself flush.

"It was hot in there, huh?" he said, looking a little flushed himself. "Shall we start in the master?"

"The rooms are all furnished?" she asked, diverting her lurid thoughts reminding her how long ago she'd had sex, let alone had a man hold her, make love to her. Was it any wonder Dylan Walker had brought out a need in her for human warmth and support? She was having a baby by herself. Not to mention the hormones coursing through her that made her more vulnerable to even a little attention from a man who was kind like Dylan.

"Ginny ordered it all and saw to the delivery. She wanted it ready when we got here."

"Even though you told her you wanted to live in the cottage for a while?"

"I'm sure she thought she could change my mind," he said under his breath.

It didn't take long to search the room—and realize that Rowena had already looked here.

"If we had some idea of what she might have been looking for," Dylan said. "Drugs? Money? Evidence?"

"Insurance maybe," Cat said, making him stop to look at her and nod.

"Insurance to keep them from ratting each other out. Maybe you're right. Maybe Ginny was trying to get out. Maybe she did go to my brother for help. I'd like to think that rather than the alternative."

They went from room to room, but Cat quickly realized the place was just too big and there were too many places to hide things. "Do you happen to have the blue-prints for this place?"

"Hoping for a secret room, stairway, compartment? Sorry, there isn't one."

"What about a safe?"

"Not that I know of. But Ginny could have had one installed, I guess. Even if she did, I wouldn't know the combination." She heard his stomach growl as they reached the bottom floor. "There's also the chance that Rowena already found it—if there was anything to find."

He shook his head. "Now that you've mentioned it, I would say she was definitely looking for something. I can see where she's been in every room of the house. I doubt she found it or I suspect she'd be gone by now. I keep thinking about you seeing her arguing with one of the FBI agents. They want something from her, ap-parently. Something maybe she hasn't been able to pro-duce."

They went through the bottom floor and found noth-ing suspicious but did find a mess in the large bedroom that Rowena was obviously using. Dylan looked at her as if to ask, "Shall we take a look through her things?"

Cat shook her head. "It wouldn't be in her things. I think we should quit. It's getting late, and I think you need to get something to eat."

He chuckled at that as they left the house and walked back toward the cottage. She'd wondered originally why he seemed to avoid the big house. Now that she knew he had planned to live there with his wife at some point and fill the place with children, it made perfect sense.

The beautiful spring evening felt as if the air was

rarified. The breeze breathed the scent of pine. Twilight cast a silver glow over them. It felt as if they were
the last two people alive. Was that why she wasn't any
more anxious to leave than he was for her to go as they
walked toward the cottage.

"You're a good listener. But you know everything
about me," he said as they neared the cottage. "I don't
know anything about you. Your baby..." He glanced at
her baby bump. "If I'm intruding just—"

"I'm having a girl."

"Congratulations. You and your husband must be excited."

She looked down at the gold band on the finger of
her left hand and then up at him before she said, "My
husband was killed in a car accident six months ago. We
were living in Libby because of his job with the forest
service. He'd been on a fishing trip on Lake Koocanusa
and heading back when he was hit by a drunk driver.
He died in the Eureka hospital. I didn't find out I was
pregnant until after he was gone. I never got the chance
to tell him."

"I'm so sorry. I should never have asked."

"It's all right. We're fine," she said smiling as she put
her hand on her stomach. "I'd just completed my law enforcement training. I was lucky there was an opening in
Fortune Creek for a pregnant newbie where there was
hardly ever any crime."

"Right." He laughed, surprised at how good it felt.
"Well, I couldn't tell you were new at this, if that helps."

"I shouldn't have admitted it."

"It's our secret. A murder though?"

She chuckled. "The truth is I was so bored I wished

for something, anything, to investigate. As they say, be careful what you wish for."

"I have complete confidence in you solving this case," he said as they reached the cottage, and he led the way into the bright kitchen.

She took a chair, realizing that she was tired.

"Stay and have dinner with me."

Was it that late? She glanced at her phone. "I completely lost track of time."

Looking up at him, she smiled. "It's just so pleasant sitting here in your kitchen. I've been on my feet all day. But I really should go."

"I swear this is why I bought this place, because of this cottage. It was love at first sight. Please stay, I really would love the company. I have steaks for the grill, vegetables for a salad, if you'll stay."

She glanced toward the front of the cottage. "What about your houseguest?"

"Seriously, you'd be doing me a huge favor. She left earlier, and I have no idea when she's coming back, but she's not invited to dinner. She was allegedly a friend of my wife's. Not mine."

"Does she know anyone in the area?" Cat asked.

"Other than Sharese and Luca, if he is in the area, I have no idea. When she leaves the ranch, I just assume she's sightseeing or gone to get a massage—at least that's what she's led me to believe. But maybe there are even more adoptees here in Montana."

"You don't trust her."

"Not any further than I can pick her up and throw her. My stomach is growling. I'm going to get dinner going if that's all right with you."

Cat told herself it was unprofessional to stay for dinner even as she said, "I'd love it, if you're sure you don't mind the company."

He left the room, returning with a small upholstered stool. "Put your feet up. I happen to love to cook and I'm sick of cooking for myself."

"I think I know why your houseguest doesn't want to leave."

"Believe me, she doesn't get this treatment. Anyway, her only interest seems to be my bar. Or whatever Ginny might have hidden in the house."

She realized she was way beyond professional ethics at this point. She'd told this man about the investigation. She'd also told him about Taylor's death, practically pouring out her entire life's history. So why didn't she feel even a twinge of guilt about that?

Because she trusted him. Because the FBI trusted him. Because she liked him, and it felt good being here with him. Even that should have made her feel guilty, but it didn't.

Not just that, it was nice out here, the pine-scented breeze blowing in through the open windows—so different from her efficient apartment over the sheriff's department. Anyway, there was little she could do back at the office. Helen would have left her post long ago. All afterhours calls to the sheriff's department were routed to Eureka's PD. They would call if she was needed.

Cat knew she was making excuses to stay because she wanted to. It felt so good sitting here with this man who was about to cook for her. He'd gone through so much. She felt a kinship with him.

She also liked watching him cook, the efficiency with

the way he worked, getting the vegetables out of the refrigerator, choosing the right size bowl and spoon before washing the produce and carefully chopping it up.

As she sat watching him make dressing for the salad, she told him about her small efficiency apartment over the sheriff's department. "I do some cooking, mostly for the baby. She's not really picky."

"When are you due, if I may ask?"

"In two months—about the time Sheriff Brandt Parker returns to take over the job again. He keeps extending his honeymoon. I'm beginning to wonder if he's ever coming back."

"How'd you meet your husband?" he asked, slicing a cucumber with a precision that awed her.

"Boy next door, same babysitter when we were little, same teachers at school." She shrugged. "We'd just always been together. It was…comfortable."

He stopped making the salad to look at her. "It sounds nice."

"It was. I miss him."

"I'm sure you do," Dylan said. "Especially now."

She put a hand over her baby bump and felt her daughter practicing her soccer moves. "We'd been married since college. We always thought we'd have kids someday. Our lives were so busy, we weren't worried when I didn't get pregnant. We thought we had time."

He looked away as if he didn't know what to say. "I'm going to get the grill going."

"I'm sorry, I didn't mean to make you uncomfortable," she said quickly.

"No, it's just that I wanted what you had with your husband, and I thought that's what I was getting with

Ginny." He shook his head. "After her death, I found
out she'd been lying to me about probably everything."

"I'm sorry," Cat said. "That has to have left you with
a lot of mixed emotions."

He laughed. "That's what these feelings are? On top
of that, the prosecutor is reopening the car bombing investigation. Not that I think it was ever really closed
since they never found out who did it. Finding out that
my brother had a baby boy who's missing… It's a lot.
I'm not sure how I feel about anything right now. Except
steaks," he said brightening. "How do you like yours?"

"Rare."

"A woman after my own heart."

He headed out the back door. Cat leaned back and
shut her eyes. She felt herself relax to the point that she
could have fallen asleep if the front door hadn't banged
open and Rowena stormed into the kitchen.

"Well, isn't this cozy," she said, frowning at Cat. "So
where is he?"

"Outside lighting the grill."

Rowena glanced at the salad bowl and the plates Dylan
had placed on the counter. "What is this?" she demanded.

"Dinner." Cat caught the smell of alcohol wafting off
the woman. "It got late. Dylan was worried about me
and the baby not getting dinner." Why was she explaining herself? Because it had felt a little too intimate? Because she liked Dylan and shouldn't, since officially he
could still be considered a suspect? Or because she'd let
herself enjoy being around another man after Taylor had
only been gone six months?

"You and the baby," Rowena said with what sounded
like disgust. "Dylan has always wanted one of those.

Too bad you're married and unavailable. I can tell he likes you."

The back door slammed as he returned. "What are you doing here, Rowena?" he said, barely giving her a glance.

"I live here," she snapped.

"You're a guest of mine in the other house," he said and gave her a get-a-clue face. "You're lucky the acting sheriff doesn't arrest you for driving under the influence. I suggest you walk to the house, so she doesn't have to."

Rowena stood there for a moment glaring daggers at the two of them before storming out.

"Whatever her reason for still being here, I don't like it, but at least here, I can keep an eye on her. There has to be a reason she's in Montana other than what she's told me." he said, taking down a platter, then pulling the steaks from the refrigerator to season them.

Cat felt the same way. "I wish we knew what she'd been looking for over at the house, but I wouldn't ignore her interest in you."

He turned to look at her, then out the window. "That's just a front for what she's really after." With that he headed out back, promising to return with a beautifully cooked steak for her.

Cat considered that. She thought it was jealousy that had made Rowena threaten Athena. Now she suspected differently. Just because Cat had seen her with one of the FBI agents also didn't mean Rowena wasn't capable of murder.

Five women and one man with at least one thing in common—their Russian births and adoptions. Two were now dead, Ginny Cooper Walker and Athena Grant.

Patty Cooper was missing and so was Athena's infant son. What were the chances that Rowena knew where they could find both Patty and the baby? And now Sharese Harmon and her brother Luca might be involved? Was it possible one of them had the baby?

Cat closed her eyes, her head aching as she tried to make sense of it all. Tomorrow she would tell the DCI team about Sharese and her brother. She almost hoped they would find Patty and, fingers crossed, the baby. She kept thinking about that little infant boy, worrying about him. What seemed like only seconds later, Dylan touched her shoulder waking her up. She felt electricity arc through her at his touch. She sat up to the stomach-growling scent of grilled steak.

"Hungry?" he asked. When he smiled like that, he was even more handsome. She felt a hard tug on her heartstrings as heat raced to her center. She'd loved her husband. But he'd never made her feel the way she was feeling right now.

"Starved," she said, realizing how true it was—and not just for dinner.

Chapter Twelve

It was late by the time Cat drove home. Dylan had tried to get her to stay. He had no idea how badly she wanted to, but not in one of his many guest bedrooms.

She felt as if she'd already stepped over a boundary she shouldn't have as acting sheriff. Worse was where she'd let her thoughts—let alone her desires—go during dinner.

She felt like a schoolgirl with her first crush and was embarrassed by it. She had to remind herself that she was seven months pregnant, a recent widow and acting sheriff. She had no business feeling these emotions, let alone these desires.

Yet, she did feel them. Worse, she fantasized about fulfilling them—if she wasn't seven months pregnant, a recent widow and acting sheriff.

Dylan had proven to be a wonderful host—and a very good cook. Her steak was perfect. She'd had him write down his salad dressing recipe for her since she'd wanted to lick her bowl it was so good.

Once in her small apartment, she checked her messages, then showered and was about to get in bed when Taylor's sister called. She and Lilly had always been like sisters. Cat told her about tonight. "I feel so guilty."

"No," her friend said. "Taylor wouldn't want you to. Anyway, I know he wasn't the love of your life. You're young. You haven't found him yet, and when you do, you go for it, Cat. You deserve to find that kind of love, passionate, crazy, no-holds-barred love."

"Wait a minute," she said laughing. "Lilly? Are we still talking about me? Or about you now? Have you found yours?"

"Well, if I did, what would you say?"

"I'd say go for it." They both laughed. "Okay, now tell me all about it."

An hour later, Cat finally crawled into bed smiling to herself because her sister-in-law had fallen head over heels in love and she couldn't be happier for her.

She must have fallen right to sleep because the next thing she knew she was jolted from a very erotic, wonderful dream to the ringing of the phone.

Picking up, she barely got out, "Acting Sheriff Cat Jameson," before JP interrupted her.

"We got another one."

She tried to clear her head. "Another one what?"

"Dead body."

Her heart in her throat, Cat said, "Not the—"

"Baby? No, sorry," JP said quickly. "An adult male, no identification on him or the female, murdered with him. What is it about you?" he asked. "Three murders in a matter of days? It's a regular crime spree."

Cat disconnected, fully awake, her mind racing. She felt goose bumps ripple over her skin. What was going on?

She got out of bed and moved to the front window to look out across the street at the hotel. The alley where she'd seen Rowena arguing with one of the agents was empty. The SUV the two feds had been driving was gone. Would they be back when they heard about two more murders?

She feared that she was on her own as she dressed and headed for the murder scene—this one along the Yaak River, not far from the Canadian border. Her daughter was kicking up a storm by the time she pulled over alongside the other law enforcement vehicles and got out.

The bodies had been dumped much like Athena Grant's and not far from the road. With all these places to bury remains, she could only assume whoever killed them had either wanted them to be found or didn't care that they would be.

"Any ID on them?" she asked when she saw JP.

He shook his head. "Want to take a look?" He glanced at her baby bump as if worried she wasn't up to this.

"Yes," she said emphatically. Both bodies had been retrieved from the ditch and now lay in body bags on two stretchers. JP unzipped first the female's. Cat braced herself, afraid she was going to recognize the woman. If was a relief when she didn't.

"Shot the same way?" she asked, and JP grunted as he re-zipped the bag and reached for the male's bag. As the zipper came down, she felt a shock. "I know this one. He's FBI." She could feel JP staring at her in surprise. "I saw him across the street from the sheriff's department arguing with a woman—not this one, someone else."

"You're sure he's FBI?" JP asked.

"I saw them when they checked into the hotel in Fortune Creek. They paid me a visit the other morning, and I saw their credentials."

"Well, it should make identifying him easier," the coroner said. "Let's get them both back to the morgue. I'll send prints right away and let you know."

On the way back to Fortune Creek, she finally admitted to herself that she was in over her head. She put in the call to the DCI and got crime team leader Hank Ferguson on the phone. She quickly updated him on the situation. He promised to send a couple of investigators, but also to keep her in the loop. Cat thanked him and barely got disconnected when Dylan called.

"I've had my people looking for Patty Cooper Harper. I have a lead down in Kalispell. Thought you might want to go with me to check it out. If she has my nephew— Well, I might need an officer of the law with me," he said.

She chuckled. "I suspect you can handle yourself in most situations."

"I hear hesitation in your voice."

"It's not that. I just turned the case and the new one over to DCI. They are sending investigators."

"Great, so you're free to follow a lead," he said. "I promise I won't step on your toes, Sheriff. Except maybe when we're slow dancing. Thought we should take my pickup—your patrol SUV kind of stands out in a crowd. Pick you up at your office?"

She thought of Helen and her eagle eyes and sharp tongue. "Better if I come to you out at the ranch since it's on the way. See you soon." She didn't mention that she was already on the road. Or that there had been two more murders. That they were killed in the same way Athena was told her the cases were connected.

But what that had to do with Dylan's nephew, she

had no idea. She suspected the baby hadn't been part of the plan and was now a problem. She just hoped he wasn't disposable.

DYLAN WAS SURPRISED how much he had been looking forward to the trip to Kalispell with Cat. He had a good feeling they were getting closer to finding his nephew. Yesterday had been the best day he'd spent at the ranch. While he loved his horseback rides, he realized now that he'd been lonely, which surprised him. He'd thought he wanted and needed to be alone so he could deal with everything.

He'd spent months dwelling in the past, blaming himself for everything that had happened and trying to understand why he hadn't seen it coming. How could he not blame himself for marrying Ginny so quickly? He had to take some responsibility for the tragedies that had followed.

Learning what he had about Ginny and the others, gave him hope that he could find out the truth and finally put the past behind him. But nothing had made him feel more hopeful than Cat. Look what she'd been through, was still going through, and how she was dealing with it.

He admired her courage and conviction. Hell, he thought with a laugh as he waited for her to buzz in at the gate, he was half in love with her, as ridiculous as it sounded even to him. But he hadn't been able to even think about the future before she'd come into his miserable existence.

Minutes later, he buzzed her in and went out on the deck to wait for her. He had a good feeling about today. With luck they would be at least one step closer to finding his nephew and making sure he was safe. He couldn't imagine going through this without Cat.

CAT SETTLED INTO the seat of Dylan's pickup as he drove off the ranch. It was one of those breathtaking Montana days in the spring when the sky was so blue it almost hurt to look at it. Not a cloud scudded across that big sky. The air smelled so good, Cat wanted to bottle it. She smiled, aware that this was the first day in a long time that she'd felt this good.

"What are you smiling about?" Dylan asked, a laugh in his voice.

"This day, being here…with you and following this lead to Patty Cooper," she said, glancing at him. "I just have a good feeling that she has the baby, that he's safe and that we're getting closer to finding him. I also feel like we're running away. It's a nice feeling. Playing hooky. I should feel guilty, but I turned the investigation over to the state crime investigators. I know when I'm out of my league."

"You do seem freer," he said, "but I can't imagine you walking away completely. You're good at your job. Don't sell yourself short."

She chuckled at that. "And you just met me a matter of days ago. But you're right. I'm still working the case, but it's good to admit when you're in over your head and let the seasoned professionals take over. There were two more murders last night. One of those murdered was an FBI agent. I'm sure they'll get involved now, as well as DCI."

"Two more murders?" He raised a brow. "Are the cases connected?"

"They were killed the same way Athena was, so I'd say yes."

"I just hope we can find Patty and my nephew. After that, let the FBI at it," he said, and she agreed.

"Tell me about this lead you have," she said as they passed Whitefish.

"I called around to motels, giving them a description of Patty and saying she might have had an infant with her. I also had a few friends involved doing the same thing."

"And you got a hit," Cat said, surprised. She and the deputies from other departments hadn't had any luck. But then again, they hadn't had a good description of Patty, while Dylan had met her at his wedding.

"Actually, the woman I spoke to said she was glad I called. She was wondering who to contact about the car. It seems Patty left the car with the license plate number she'd put down on her motel registration form in their parking lot."

Cat shook her head in awe. "Nice work." He would have made a good cop. While she didn't know exactly what work he'd done outside his career, he'd made it sound as if it had been for the government So, she shouldn't have been surprised, but he kept exceeding her expectations.

Once at the hotel, Cat introduced herself to the manager who led them out to the car parked at the far side of the parking lot. It was a nondescript sedan with Montana plates, probably a rental that hadn't been picked up yet. Patty had either been picked up by someone else or had the rental agency bring her another car. Maybe they had planned to come back for this one.

Dylan pulled a device from behind the seats of his pickup that looked like a metal ruler only thinner. It took him only a few seconds to unlock the car. By then Cat had pulled on a pair of latex gloves. She'd learned to always carry several pairs in her business.

The first thing she saw was the blood on the passenger side seat. For a moment, she was taken aback, especially when she saw what looked like a wadded-up bloody baby blanket on the floor. The interior had a smell that threatened to turn her stomach. She made the call to DCI team leader Hank Ferguson so they could get a forensics team to go over the car. Then she finished searching the inside.

When she got ready to check the trunk, she hesitated. Dylan met her gaze. "You want me to do it?" he asked.

She shook her head and braced herself, afraid of what she would find. As the trunk lid yawned open, she saw with relief that it was empty. "Athena wasn't killed in the car," Cat said as she slammed the trunk lid. "But I suspect she was transported in it before she was killed and dumped along the road. It would explain the blood on the passenger seat and floorboard. Have to wait until forensics finishes with it to know for sure."

She looked toward the hotel, thinking of Patty and the baby. Where were they now? Patty could have taken him out of Montana, maybe even out of the country. Unless there was a reason she had to stay around here.

"Why didn't she leave the area right away?" Cat asked herself out loud. "She had to know that everyone would be looking for the baby once Athena's body was found. Why stay?"

Dylan shook his head. "Is she waiting for Rowena to go with them?"

"Maybe," she said as she walked to his pickup and climbed in. "I'll make sure the FBI gets photos of Patty and Rowena in case they decide to skip the country with the baby."

Her cell rang. Checking, she saw it was JP. She picked up.

"He wasn't FBI," the coroner said without preamble.

She knew at once he was talking about the man who'd been murdered the night before. "Then who is he?"

"A Russian geologist over here on a student visa," JP said. "At least that's how he got the visa. The real FBI have been notified."

"And the woman?"

"Nothing yet. I heard you turned the cases over to the DCI."

"It was time," Cat said. "I'm still working the case, though. I needed help."

"Smart decision," he said. She thought she heard pride in his voice. "You've done good." With that he was gone.

She disconnected, feeling a little better. She admired and respected JP, so a compliment from him was worth gold.

"You're not giving up," Dylan said, then looked over at her having obviously heard enough of the conversation to read between the lines. "Calling in reinforcements is just good business."

Cat had to smile even as she fought tears. She wasn't as upset about messing up with the counterfeit FBI agents as she was in what it meant. The men who'd posed as FBI agents said they had no interest in Dylan, and she'd taken their word for him no longer being a suspect in the case.

"But no one should count you out."

She nodded, but she wasn't all that sure that her judgment wasn't flawed—especially when it came to Dylan Walker. She'd taken the word of a man posing as an FBI agent that Dylan Walker could be trusted. Had she jumped at it because she'd wanted to believe it? Because she liked him. More than liked him.

"I should probably get back," she said, hand going to her stomach to feel her daughter moving around. To remind her what was at stake. She couldn't make this about herself. She'd never been able to. She took a couple of deep breaths.

"Anything you want to talk about?" Dylan asked as they climbed into his pickup.

She thought about just brushing it off as "work stuff" but stopped herself as he began to drive through town toward the road that would take them back to his ranch. "Those two FBI agents I told you about? They weren't agents. The one who's dead was a Russian here on a student visa."

Dylan said nothing for a moment. "Now you're thinking of me again as a suspect." He met her gaze. "What do you want to know?"

"Did you leave the ranch last night?"

"No. Can anyone substantiate that? No. I didn't see Rowena's car when I went to bed. I have no idea what time she came in, but she was back this morning when I left. I haven't talked to her."

"What about your gate intercom system? Does it keep track of visitors?"

He chuckled at that. "Before you and Rowena showed up, I hadn't had any visitors for three months so no reason to install a video camera that recorded every wild animal that walked past."

"I don't mean to sound—"

"Suspicious? But you are and that's okay. I don't mind."

She didn't believe that. He looked hurt. She thought about how happy he'd looked when he'd picked her up. She hated that she'd taken that away from him. While she wanted to tell him that she trusted him, she wasn't sure she could right now.

Cat looked out her side window, thinking what a long ride it would be on the way back to Fortune Creek. She was wishing there was something she could say when she spotted Rowena on a side street.

"Stop!" she ordered Dylan. He hit his brakes and pulled over, no doubt hearing the alarm in her voice. She was already getting out as she said, "It's Rowena coming out of what appears to be a baby shop."

DYLAN SWORE. Cat was out of the pickup almost before he got it fully stopped, but he wasn't far behind her. Ahead he could see Rowena carrying a shopping bag with a children's shop logo on it. She slowed, then stopped to take a phone call as they approached her from behind.

All Dylan heard her say into the phone was, "I'm doing the best I can. You yelling at me isn't helping." Rowena looked alarmed and instantly disconnected when she saw the two of them. "What are you doing here?"

"I want to ask you the same thing," the sheriff said. "Been doing some baby shopping?"

Rowena pulled the bag closer to herself. "My niece just had a baby. I was getting her a present."

"Girl or boy?" Cat said, grabbing the top of the bag and pulling it open enough to see what the woman had bought. "A boy, huh? Where is Athena Grant's baby?"

"Who?"

"Don't play dumb," Dylan snapped. "Where is my nephew?"

Rowena looked around nervously as if afraid someone was watching them. "I don't know what you're talking about."

"Murder is what we're talking about and kidnapping," Cat said. "I'm worried about that baby's safety. I think it's time you told me what's going on."

Rowena shook her head and tried to walk around them, but Dylan grabbed her arm. "Enough games. I want my nephew."

"You have no idea what you've gotten involved in," the woman said through gritted teeth as she again looked around, even more nervous now as she pulled free.

"Where were you taking these baby clothes?" Cat demanded. "You need to take us to the baby."

"I told you, they're for my niece's new baby."

"You're lying," Dylan said. "If anything happens to my nephew—"

"The FBI is now involved," Cat said. "The *real* FBI. I saw you talking to a man a couple of nights ago who was pretending to be an agent, but he's now dead, along with an older woman who was with him." She saw surprise on Rowena's face followed quickly by fear.

"Don't threaten me," Rowena snapped looking cornered. "Either of you. You have no idea." She took a step backward, then another.

"Rowena—"

"Arrest me or leave me alone." With that she turned and hurried down the street.

"She knows I don't have enough evidence to arrest her," Cat said. "But let's try to follow her."

Unfortunately, by the time they got back to his pickup, Rowena was gone.

"At least she's buying clothes for the baby," Cat said, her voice breaking.

Dylan pulled over in a residential area under a large weeping willow tree. He cut the engine and turned to look at her. "I hate that you don't trust me now."

The large tree formed a canopy over them, cocooning them in dark shade away from the rest of the world. "I didn't say—"

"You don't have to. I can see it in your eyes. Cat…" He seemed at a loss for words for a few moments. "Right or wrong, I started caring about you. If this case is as dangerous as it appears—and Rowena claims, maybe you should distance yourself from it—and from me. Otherwise…" He reached over, his fingers trailing down her bare arm from the elbow to the wrist before pulling back.

"I can't do that, not from the case…not from you," she said as she met his gaze and held it. "I've never felt…"

"Like this?" He nodded. "I've never wanted anyone the way I do you."

WAS THIS REAL? Cat couldn't believe it. She let out a laugh that was close to a sob. She'd wanted to feel like this her whole life, this kind of all-consuming passion, this desire that made her feel more alive than she'd ever felt. Now that she did meet someone who stoked those fires of desire, she was *pregnant*.

"A woman seven months pregnant?" she cried.

"You couldn't be more desirable than you are right now." He leaned toward her, gently cupping the back of her head with his hand as he kissed her at first gently, then with growing passion. Her mouth opened to his in a wordless surrender as she dug her fingers into his strong shoulders.

She felt her nipples pebble, pressing hard against her bra. Her pulse thundered in her ears, an ache of longing in her chest that shot all the way to her center. She told herself this wasn't her, yet she knew this had been the missing part of her for years, the passionate unfulfilled part of her she'd unconsciously dreamed of.

"We can't go back to my place or yours," he said as he pulled back, sounding breathless. His gaze held hers. "I know somewhere we can go."

Was she really doing this? She nodded.

Dylan kept his hand on her leg as he drove. Cat spent the short drive trying to talk some sense into herself. She didn't have to go through with this. He would understand. Stopping this before it got started was the sensible thing to do.

She'd spent her life being sensible. Isn't that why she'd married Taylor? Because it was the sensible, safe thing to do. She'd known that he loved her, she'd known him practically her whole life. There would be no surprises. Even the first time they made love had been comfortable—expected. They'd been inseparable as friends for years. Of course, there hadn't been fireworks or passion. There had been companionship, safety, a predictable life.

Except a drunk driver had taken that away and now here she was, pregnant with Taylor's baby about to do what?

She looked over at Dylan. The way her heart was pounding she felt as if she was about to leap off a cliff. She was definitely about to leave her comfort zone and careen into the unknown. Her pulse pounded at the thought as Dylan pulled up in front of a beautiful house overlooking Flathead Lake.

"It's my brother Beau's," he said and cut the engine. "He's the reason I bought the ranch out here."

Chapter Thirteen

Her legs felt weak, her heart a hammer against her ribs, as Dylan opened her door and helped her out of his truck as if they were on a date. That sensible side of her kept yelling *Stop! You don't know this man. This isn't you.*

No, it wasn't her and there was something liberating about that. But why now? Why under these circumstances, seven months pregnant in the middle of a triple murder investigation?

Because life threw curves. It had taken Taylor. It had brought Dylan Walker into her life. All he had to do was look at her and she went weak with desire. She wanted desperately to see where he could take her. Her instincts told her she was in for a wild ride, one that her old self had secretly longed for.

He found the key where it was hidden and opened the door. She barely noticed the spectacular view of the lake with the sunlight on the clear water or the array of colored rocks shimmering beneath. The scent of pine and water followed her inside the cool darkness of the house.

She turned as Dylan came in the door behind her. She hadn't known what she was going to say until the words came off her lips. "I trust you."

He looked at her, his gaze on hers as if searching for the truth before he smiled and took her in his arms. The kiss was a promise even before he said the words, as if he could tell that she was scared on so many levels. "We won't do anything you don't want to do. Nor will we do anything that might harm the baby, I promise." Then he swung her up into his arms and, kissing her, carried her deeper into the house.

Dylan broke the kiss to lay her down on a huge bed that seemed to float in front of the window overlooking the lake. She pulled him down next to her.

"I love looking into those eyes of yours," he whispered as his hand cupped her cheek. "I saw your intelligence the first day I met you. I was a little intimidated by it. I still am."

She chuckled and shook her head. "Did you know we were going to end up here today?"

"No. If you're asking if I planned this, definitely not. I had no ulterior motives asking you to come with me today. Except that I wanted you with me."

"When did you know you wanted this?" she asked, her gaze holding his.

"When I saw how hard it was for you to ask the state crime team for help, when I saw how it hurt you. I wanted to make you feel better. I love your smile and wanted the ability to put it back where it belonged."

"And now you think you have that ability?"

He blinked. *"You're challenging me?"* He laughed, smiling down at her. "You want me to prove it." She nodded and kissed him seductively, feeling nothing like her old self. She didn't know this woman, but she wanted to get to.

Dylan took that challenge as he deepened the kiss, burying his fingers in her hair, pulling it free to fall around her shoulders. Shivers of desire rippled over her skin. His skill reminded her of how long it had been since a man had made love to her.

Just the thought of her husband brought with it a deep sorrow. She'd told herself and Dylan that she and Taylor hadn't had children because they'd been too busy. Now she could admit that they had been growing apart from the years together. They hardly ever made love, both involved more in other things than each other.

Dylan pushed her over onto her back. He met her gaze, holding it. She nodded and smiled, even as he noticed what she hadn't. He wiped a tear from her cheek with his thumb. "Is it too soon?"

She shook her head and pulled him down for another kiss. This time when he pulled back, he seemed to see the desire in her eyes, the need, and the pain that came with that naked need.

He kissed her behind her ear, then trailed kisses down her throat. As he did, he unbuttoned her shirt. Goose bumps rippled over her flesh as he met her gaze and drew out her right breast. Bending over it he sucked the taut nipple into his mouth, making her moan as desire shot through her.

She wanted this. Wanted it desperately. She arched against him as he withdrew her left breast, and pressing them together, sucked her nipples into hard, aching points. She moaned, her hands cupping his head and he worked his way further south. His tongue trailed down over her stomach to the V.

Again, he looked at her as if waiting for permission.

She spread her legs, making him smile as he slid further down the bed and lifted her. His tongue tentatively touched the aching part of her. Cat could hear herself as she writhed to the movement of his tongue, her moans growing louder and louder until she cried out as the intense release came in waves of pleasure. Gasping for breath, she drew him back up to her and started to unbutton his shirt, when his hands stopped her.

She looked up into his face. Her heart was still pounding, her body weak and still vibrating with the intensity of her climax. She met his gaze in a questioning one of her own.

Dylan shook his head. "Maybe next time, if there is one. This time was about you." He pulled her into his arms and held her close. She pressed her face into his warm shoulder, torn between laughing and crying.

"That was…" She couldn't even formulate words.

"That was just foreplay, Cat," he said with a laugh, then pulled back a little to look at her. "Was there anyone other than your husband?"

She shook her head and waited for him to ask if Taylor had ever… "Not like that," she said, burying her face again. She felt him chuckle.

"Glad I could be the first. Do you mind?" he asked as he put his hand on her belly. His eyes lit up as her daughter gave him her version of a high five. "She all right?"

"We are both more than all right. I can have sex, you know. We just have to be careful."

Dylan nodded. "Like I said, maybe next time." He drew her close again.

Cat felt as if she could stay right there forever. The sunlight on the lake threw shadows on the coffered ceiling of the bedroom. "This is your brother's place? I guess I'm surprised you still have it." She felt his hesitation before he finally spoke.

"I haven't been able to sell it."

Her cell rang. She pulled away just far enough to reach her phone where it had fallen out of her jeans. It was JP.

"I'm sorry," she said to Dylan. "I need to—"

"Do your job," he said smiling as he swung his legs over the side of the bed. "I would expect nothing less of you. I'll give you some privacy." He left the room. Cat answered the call.

"If you tell me that there's been another murder," she said as she reached to pick up her discarded clothing, not even remembering when it had come off.

"Thought you'd want to know. We have an ID on the dead woman found with the bogus fed. Her name is Lindsey Martin. Isn't that the name the pregnant woman gave you?"

"It is. It's her mother's maiden name."

He let out a low whistle. "No doubt the cases are connected, is there."

"No," she said. "But we still don't know what's going on or who else is involved. At least now DCI is on it." She'd told them what she'd found out about the adoptions and the women involved. They knew as much as she did now.

"So, you're still working the case?" JP asked. "I got a call about you finding a car connected with a woman named Patty Cooper. The lab did a preliminary test on the blood found on the passenger seat. It's Athena Grant's."

"I suspected it would be." She'd managed to get dressed as she talked.

"The FBI is involved as well, but I probably don't have to tell you that."

"Guess they all have it covered." She'd never quit anything in her life. Wasn't that why she was having a hard time with this? Just like she would have never thought of leaving Taylor. But life's curve had her husband gone, her pregnant and now passing off her first job and falling for one of her former suspects. "I have to go, JP. Thanks for letting me know."

She hung up and turned to see Dylan standing in the doorway. From just the expression on his face, she knew something was wrong. Then she saw a man she recognized behind him. The second fake FBI man was holding a gun to Dylan's head.

Cat could see her own weapon out of the corner of her eye. It lay on the bedside table almost within reach. But Dylan saw her look in its direction and gave a slight shake of his head.

DYLAN HAD BEEN trained in hand-to-hand combat. But the moment he'd seen the man holding the gun and realized he wasn't alone, Dylan wasn't going to take a chance with Cat's life and that of her baby's. He hoped that wasn't a mistake.

Now he just had to keep Cat from doing anything dangerous until they found out what was going on. Clearly, they'd been followed. If he hadn't been so anxious to get to his brother's lake house and make love with the acting sheriff, he would have been more careful. Then again, it had been a while since he'd had to worry about being followed—let alone killed. He was out of practice. He'd thought when he moved out here that he'd never have to worry about watching for a tail again.

"Someone wants to talk to us," he said carefully to Cat. "It appears we have little choice, so let's hear what he has to say."

"Without your weapon, please, Sheriff," the man said. He motioned her into the living room where she and Dylan were ordered to sit on the loveseat and not move. Dylan reached over and took her hand, squeezing it gently, hoping to reassure her.

The man who'd been standing by the door stepped forward. He was tall, slim and dressed in a suit that spoke of authority. He introduced himself as Brian Fuller, an officer with the regional intelligence agency as he took a seat on a chair across from them.

"Intelligence? I'd like to see some identification," Cat said. "No offense, but your associate presented himself as FBI and isn't, and now he's holding a gun on us, making it hard to believe that either of you are who you say you are."

Fuller smiled. "Jason is homeland security. If it makes you more comfortable, I'll have him put his weapon away." He pulled out his credentials and tossed it to Dylan. "I believe Mr. Walker is familiar with my type of identification." Dylan felt Cat watching him as he studied the ID, then tossed it back.

"You followed us here, your associate broke in and held a gun to my head," Dylan said. "Is that the way your office operates?"

Fuller sighed. "I shouldn't have to tell you that we use any means available to us when necessary. Sorry for the unpleasant tactics, but I need to ask you both a few questions, especially you, Mr. Walker, about your… friend, Rowena Keeling, and I wanted to do it in private."

Dylan didn't hesitate. "She's not my friend. She's an unwelcome houseguest who's been detained in the area because of the recent murders."

"I have a few questions myself," Cat said, speaking up. "You wouldn't be here unless you knew more about what was going on than we do. Who killed Athena Grant and her adoptive mother?"

"I'm sorry, Sheriff Jameson, but I'm asking the questions," Fuller said. "How long have you and Mr. Walker known each other?"

"In other words, you want to know how much we already know," Dylan said. "Ms. Jameson and I met after Athena tried to contact me, and failing, she went to the sheriff for help." Fuller nodded. "Since then, we discovered four women who were born in Russia, adopted to parents living in Denver, who we believe became friends—or at least seem to be in league together—including possibly my deceased wife. We also only recently found two more Russian-born adoptions out of Missoula. We believe they might be spying for Russia."

Fuller sat back in his chair, his expression giving nothing away.

"We are right, aren't we," Cat said. "Is your agency responsible for killing them?"

"We don't operate that way, Sheriff Jameson."

"Do you know where Athena's baby is?" Cat asked him.

"I'm sorry, I do not at this point," Fuller said.

"Are you telling us we're right and that they are Russian spies?" she asked. "Part of a sleeper cell?"

"He's obviously trying really hard not to tell us anything," Dylan said.

Fuller smiled at that. "It's true, the Russian traditional counterintelligence threat continues to loom large in our country. Spies live among us. We estimate there are one hundred thousand foreign agents from not just Russia, but other countries as well, spying on us. Washington, DC, has more spies than any other world city. Often the way we catch them is a tip from a friend or spouse."

Dylan felt Cat's gaze shift to him as he asked, "Are you saying my wife came to you?"

Fuller sighed. "I can't reveal my source."

"Wait, you're saying you were aware of what was going on?" Cat asked.

"That's our job," the officer said. "We've been trying to find the people responsible for the car bombing that killed your brother and wife, but also find out why."

"Was Ginny double-crossing her friends?" Dylan asked.

Fuller looked tight-lipped. "We focus on specific priorities. State agencies, the military and companies working on sensitive technologies as prime targets for foreign espionage." His gaze met Dylan's. "And protecting our asset."

"I'm no longer one of your assets," he said.

"No, but we believe you were caught up in a honeytrap operation," Fuller said and turned to Cat. "Honeytrap operations use sexpionage by a foreign female agent known as a sparrow to compromise an opponent sexually to elicit information."

Dylan swore. "If you think that is what Rowena Keeling is doing—" Cooper Walker, the man said.

"What are you talking about?" he demanded.

"We have it on good authority that Ginny Cooper obtained the names of those we have working in the same capacity you did during your years of service. She was threatening to expose them—and you—when she was killed."

Chapter Fourteen

Cat saw Dylan's flushed face as he shot to his feet. "You can't believe I gave her any such list."

Jason brandished his weapon again but Fuller waved him back.

"Calm down, Mr. Walker. We believe your wife got her hands on the list for her native-born country from some-one close to you," he said.

For a moment he looked confused, then he swore. "My brother, Beau," Dylan said, his voice rough with anger.

"We don't know that for a fact, Mr. Walker."

"Then what do you know?" Dylan demanded angrily. "Was it my brother?"

Fuller turned to Cat. "Have you ever heard of the Moscow Rules of spying, Sheriff Jameson? *Assume nothing. Never go against your gut. Everyone is potentially under opposition control. Do not look back: you are never completely alone. Go with the flow, blend in. Vary your pattern and stay within your cover.* Those rules are posted in the International Spy Museum in Washington, DC."

"I don't understand," she said, more than a little confused.

"We are dealing with a different breed of Russian

spies. Spies usually have contact with no one else, never learning the names of any other spies or officials. But these Russian-born females adopted by American families either found each other—or their controller found them and activated them.

"Originally, we believe that Mr. Walker here was the mark," Fuller continued. "But your wife must have realized that you would never give up your associates. So, she found someone who would."

"How was it possible that my brother had such a list?" Dylan demanded.

"We aren't sure that he did have it, but he was apparently involved somehow because he became a target."

Dylan shook his head. "If true and the list is out there, then why hasn't the Soviet Union acted on it? Or have they?"

Fuller shook his head. "We don't believe Ginny Cooper Walker ever delivered the document to the Soviets or anyone else."

"Wasn't it possible she had it with her, and it was destroyed in the bombing?" Dylan asked.

The director shook his head. "It appears to be missing." He looked directly at Cat. "That is why people are dying. There seems to be two factions involved, one trying to get the document, the other killing people to either stop it from falling into the wrong hands or fighting for it because they've already made a deal with another country that wants it."

"And you don't know who is who," Cat finished for him.

Fuller shifted in the chair. "I understand this is your

first position in law enforcement. I hope it's not your last."

"Is that a threat?" Dylan demanded.

"Not at all. I admire Sheriff Jameson. I already knew your abilities, Mr. Walker. I find the two of you an interesting but very capable team."

"Then what is it you want?" he demanded.

"I don't want that document to fall into the wrong hands, and I suspect you don't either since your name will be on that list," Fuller said. "I also don't want the two of you to get killed since right now you are both deep in the middle of this."

"But there is something else you want," Cat said.

The director nodded and turned to Dylan. "Your wife had that document. That means it must still be in your possession, whether you're aware of it or not. Find it."

"If I do, I'll destroy it," Dylan said.

"That would be a mistake. The only way this is going to stop is if both sides know it's destroyed."

"I'll make sure they do," he promised.

Fuller sighed and got to his feet. "I would prefer that when you find it, you turn it over to me. But I understand your lack of trust in anyone other than..." His gaze swung to Cat for a moment, then back to Dylan. "I wanted to alert you both to what a dangerous position you're in."

"Which one of the women is working for you?" Cat asked. "Rowena?"

Clearly ignoring the question, the man said, "There is no shame in walking completely away from this, Sheriff Jameson, especially given your condition. I highly recommend it." With that he pulled out two business cards, handed one to Cat and another to Dylan. "You find the document, you call." He motioned to his companion and the two walked out, leaving Cat and Dylan alone.

For a moment, neither spoke. The house grew uncomfortably quiet, making Cat aware of the growing darkness outside. The sun had long ago dropped behind the mountains, leaving the lake plated in silver light. The mountains beyond the water were etched black against the pale sky. The quiet was deafening.

"You were right, Cat," Dylan said after a moment. "Rowena was looking for the document."

"But is she still looking or is she waiting for us to find it? And if so, who is she working for?"

He shook his head. "Mind if we swing by my ranch on the way home? After our run-in with Rowena, I want to see if she came back to the house."

"She has the code to get back in?"

"I haven't changed it yet. That could have been a mistake."

"You really think she went back to the ranch after we confronted her?" Cat asked.

"Yes. Unless she took all her belongings with her when she left the ranch, she has to come back for them. I don't think she'd finished. Not yet. Unless she found the document. It sure didn't sound that way with whomever she was talking to on the phone when we approached her."

After locking up the lake house, Dylan drove them to the ranch. They didn't speak on the drive. Cat assumed that like her, Dylan was going over everything they'd learned. As they pulled in through the gate and drove up the road, she spotted Rowena's SUV parked in front of the cottage. "Looks like she's changed residences."

Dylan swore and sped up. "Like hell."

As he swung into a spot next to the woman's SUV, Rowena came out of his cottage. "You really should lock your doors," she said, standing her ground as the two of them exited his pickup.

"What were you doing in there?" he demanded.

"Just left you a note," she said. "I'm leaving in the morning." Her gaze swung to Cat. "Unless you're going to arrest me. But I didn't think so."

"Get that package mailed off to your niece?" Cat said.

"As a matter of fact, I did." She eyed Cat. "They say pregnancy makes a woman glow, but I don't think that's what put that color in your cheeks, Sheriff." A big grin spread across her face before she laughed and turned to Dylan. "I saw the way you looked at her. But I have to hand it to you. Didn't take you any time at all to seduce her."

"Rowena—"

"Don't even bother, Dylan." Her gaze whipped back to Cat. "Be careful. My best friend was married to him. He is a man of many secrets. You have no idea what he's capable of. Ginny didn't either. I kept telling her to get out while she could. Too bad she didn't listen. Now she's dead." Rowena lifted a brow. "Think about that, Acting Sheriff."

"That's enough, Rowena," Dylan snapped. "Why wait until morning? Why don't you leave now?"

She smiled at him. "You're right. Why not say good-bye now." She turned to Cat. "Good luck. Too bad about your husband, Taylor Jameson, right? What a terrible accident." Cat saw something unsettling in the woman's expression. "Turns out you aren't as smart as you think you are." She turned to glare at Dylan before walking away. "Enjoy your evening. Too bad it will be your last."

"What was that about?" Cat asked, shaken by her mentioning Taylor and the wreck that killed him as she watched Rowena walk away.

"I have no idea," Dylan said. "But I'm worried that she wasn't in the cottage just to leave me a note." He headed for the door. "You might want to wait here."

What had the woman left? The baby? That thought propelled her toward the cottage door until she realized she hadn't heard a sound from inside. What if—

"Wait here," Dylan said as if thinking the same thing.

Cat couldn't bear to wait. She rushed in behind him. They didn't find the baby, alive or dead, but Rowena had left a note on his kitchen table. Dylan didn't touch it. Instead, he left to search the rest of the cottage, coming back to say he hadn't found anything out of place that he could tell.

They both looked down at the note lying on the table.

Sorry things didn't work out.

Chapter Fifteen

"What *things*?" Cat asked, turning to look at him.

"The document?" he said with a shrug.

"That's only one thing. Maybe she planned to use... what was it Fuller called it? Sexpionage. Maybe she really thought you'd fall for her."

He shook his head.

"I got the feeling that she was jealous of your wife," Cat said.

"Rowena? She had nothing to be jealous of, she was born rich and spoiled. As far as I could tell, she could have any man she wanted and she wanted a lot of them."

"Every man but you," Cat said.

"If she wanted me, it was to rub it in Ginny's face, but Ginny's gone and hopefully Rowena will be gone from here soon. Her note makes it sound as if she's giving up."

Cat shook her head. "I don't believe it. I'm wondering what her next move is. Rowena must realize that you don't have the document and since she has no idea where Ginny might have hidden it—"

"Just my luck." Dylan was shaking his head. "I agree. She's not giving up. I doubt she could if she wanted to. But maybe she wants us to believe she is." His gaze settled on her, warm and inviting. "You sure you have to go home?"

She nodded. "Are you going to be all right here with Rowena still on the property?"

"I plan to sleep with one eye open and my .45 nearby, and as soon as she's gone, I'll reset the gate so she can't get back in."

Cat couldn't tell if he was joking or not about the .45. "Seriously, be careful."

"You too. Maybe I should follow you back to Fortune Creek."

She shook her head. "I'll be fine."

He stepped toward her, hugged her and then kissed her, holding her in the warmth and strength of his arms. She didn't want to leave, but she also couldn't stay. So much had happened today. She needed time and space to try to make sense of it. She figured Dylan did too since Fuller had made it sound as if Ginny had only married him for the list.

Cat was sure that he'd already suspected that had been the case. But it was one more deception, one more lie, one more betrayal.

"When this is over..." he whispered next to her ear.

The words rushed straight to her heart. A promise of what could be. If they survived it. Cat pulled back to kiss him, then stepped from his arms to walk to her patrol SUV before she changed her mind about leaving.

It was later than she thought as she headed for Fortune Creek. She put down her window to drive slowly, letting the cold night air rush in as if it could clear her mind. She could still taste Dylan on her lips and all she could think about was being back in his arms.

She pushed the thought away, a little shocked at herself. Would Taylor be shocked as well, or would he be happy for her? She thought he would be happy but maybe a little worried that she would get her heart broken. He might also worry about their daughter. Who fell in love seven months pregnant?

At least now she knew what Rowena and the others had been looking for. But if the document wasn't hidden on the ranch, then where? She reminded herself that the ranch was over a thousand acres. Ginny could have hidden it anywhere.

Cat hadn't gone far when she spotted headlights behind her. Dylan? After she left had he gotten worried and decided to follow her home? The thought made her smile—until she noticed how quickly the vehicle was gaining on her, its headlights on high beam.

Chapter Sixteen

Dylan found himself more anxious than he'd been in months. He'd watched Cat disappear into the darkness, and he was unable to shake the gut-deep feeling that she wasn't safe. That road to Fortune Creek was narrow and winding and seldom had any traffic on it. If she broke down or had a flat, she might be stranded in the dark and cold until morning.

He grabbed his keys and headed for his pickup. No matter what she said, he was going to follow her home. He wouldn't be able to sleep if he didn't. Once past the gate, he drove as fast as the road would allow, all his instincts pushing him to catch sight of her.

As he came over a rise, he saw taillights and tried to relax. But the closer he got, the more confused he became. The lights were wrong. He wasn't following Cat's patrol SUV. Instead, it was an older farm truck with a wooden stock rack on the back. He frowned, realizing he'd seen the truck before—parked in one of the old barns on his ranch.

He felt a shock rocket through him. What the hell? Who was driving his truck? He punched the gas and tried to pull up beside the large farm vehicle, determined to find out who was driving it and if he was right about it being his.

But as he came along the driver's side almost close enough to see the driver, the truck swerved into his lane crashing into the side of his pickup and sending him flying off the road.

CAT THOUGHT FOR a moment that she saw a second set of headlights behind her, but as she dropped over a rise, both disappeared. Hurriedly she looked for a spot to pull over, but the road was narrow and hilly. There wasn't a wide spot that she could see ahead and the vehicle behind her had topped the rise and was now gaining on her quickly.

She thought about the alleged drunk driver who had killed her husband on this very road, although miles from here, closer to the Canadian border. She touched her brakes, thinking the driver just hadn't seen her, and got over to the edge of the road as far as she could to let him pass.

Except the driver didn't pass. She sped up seeing that the truck wasn't going to pass her. Blinded by the headlights, she couldn't see the driver, but she knew then what he intended to do. She thought of Fuller's warning. She'd become a problem. Dylan too.

The large truck chased after her, barreling down on her. He was gaining. Any moment he was going to crash into the back of her SUV. She gripped the wheel hard, her fingers aching as she fought to stay on the road. All she could think about was her baby. If she went off the road and into the trees—

She felt a hard jolt as the truck rammed the back

of her SUV, the back window exploding as the truck made contact. She could feel the cold night air whistling through the gaping hole. Her SUV began to fishtail. She hung onto the wheel, fighting to right the vehicle without going off the rough edge of the shoulderless road. She'd only just gained control when she looked in her rearview mirror.

The truck seemed to back off. What was the driver doing? Then she saw it. He'd only backed off to make another run at her, to increase his speed. This time he planned to hit her harder in an attempt to drive her off the road.

She had the gas pedal to the floor. She couldn't go any faster. Nor was there any place to get off this road before she was forced from it.

In her rearview mirror, she could see nothing but headlights bearing down on her. The truck was coming at her again. Her baby, she thought. She couldn't wreck. She couldn't lose her baby, her life. Not now, not when she'd glimpsed a possible bright future she'd only dreamed possible.

The truck was almost on her again, coming faster this time.

DYLAN'S PICKUP LEFT the road, soared over the shallow barrow pit before touching down hard in a field. He fought the wheel to keep control as he was still going fast. Ahead he could see a stand of pines looming in his headlights. He turned the wheel back in the direction of the road he'd just left. The ground was soft. He could feel the tires digging into the dirt as he roared back onto the road, losing control for a moment as he did.

He hadn't known this kind of fear in a very long time, if ever. He'd never had this much on the line even with his government job. This was personal. He felt responsible for Cat and her baby, for Beau's baby as well. He had to catch that truck and stop it—no matter what he had to do.

In the distance, he could see the taillights of the truck. He didn't kid himself that the driver of the truck had accidently forced him off the road. Where was Cat? If it had been an accident or he'd been the intended target, the truck driver would have stopped. Which meant the intended target was up the road. *Cat.*

The thought sent his pulse racing as he sped after the truck. At the top of the hill, he saw two sets of taillights ahead. The truck was right behind Cat's SUV, barreling down on it. Dylan had no doubt what the driver planned to do. He floored his pickup. The right front tire scraped loudly on the dented panel where the truck had slammed into him. But otherwise, the pickup was still running fine.

Gaining on the truck, Dylan pulled out his gun. His hand shook for a moment. While he could shoot with either his left or his right hand with accuracy, he hadn't been to a firing range in months.

He calmed those thoughts, telling himself that he had to get close enough to make a decent shot. He put down his window, letting the cold spring night air rush in to clear his head and strengthen his focus.

Dylan took aim. He couldn't let the truck drive Cat's SUV off the road, not in this hilly area filled with trees and a creek at the bottom of the steepest of the hills to his right. But if he didn't stop the driver of the truck—

CAT GRIPPED THE wheel as the inside of the SUV filled again with the lights from the big truck. She braced herself for the impact, terrified what would happen if she crashed, especially at this speed. Just the thought of the airbag exploding and harming her daughter—

She shoved her seat as far back as she could and still reach the pedals. She would have disabled the airbag if she could have—concerned only for her baby.

The truck was so close now, she could hear the roar of its engine. The headlights filled her vehicle, the sound through the broken window at the back deafening. Gripping the wheel, she looked back, but could only see the front end of the huge old truck about to take away everything from her.

Braced for impact, she hadn't realized that she'd been holding her breath when suddenly the truck behind her began to swerve wildly. The sound of the truck's big engine seemed to die as she heard the squeal of brakes. The truck was rocking precariously, the headlights wavering. An instant later, the headlights veered to the right as the truck went crashing off the road and disappeared down a hillside.

That's when she saw the lights of the other vehicle behind her. That driver had hit his brakes. As she slowed her SUV to a stop, she could no longer hold back the flood of emotions. Hugging her belly, she began to sob. She'd told herself that she knew the dangers that went with being an officer of the law. But it had never hit home like it did at that moment. She could have lost her baby tonight. She could have lost everything.

WEAK WITH RELIEF, Dylan jumped out of his pickup and rushed to Cat's SUV. He saw her hugging herself. As he approached, his flashlight in one hand, his weapon in the other, he saw her tears and knew that they weren't for herself, but for her baby. She unlocked her door and stumbled out and into his arms. "Thank you for whatever you did," she said, her voice breaking. She didn't have to tell him how frightened she'd been. He could feel it in her hug, see it in her red tear-streaked face, hear it in her voice.

"Shot out the rear left tire." She nodded, still leaning into him. "You're all right," he whispered as he held her. "I need to go down the hill and check the truck. Stay here. The driver might come back up the hill to the road. Don't take a chance. Shoot the SOB."

She nodded, wiping at her tears. "I'm okay." Her hand went to her belly. "We're all right."

"You certainly are. I'll be back." He saw her reach for her service revolver and knew that she was indeed okay again, the scare over. At least for now.

With that he dropped over the hill, shining the flashlight beam into the darkness. The hill was steep, ending in a stand of pines next to a creek. He could see the truck's taillights glowing deep in the grove and smelled the scent of burned oil and leaking radiator fluid on the night air.

As he drew closer, he saw that the driver's side door was standing open. He slowed, pocketing the flashlight to ready the gun. Darkness hunkered in the trees along the creek. He could hear and smell the water, mixing with the smells of the wrecked truck. What he didn't hear was anyone moving inside the vehicle.

Working along the side of the large truck, he made his way to the open driver's side door. Taking a breath, he waited then peered around the edge of the open door to look inside.

Just as he'd expected, in the ambient light of the headlights, he could see that the cab was empty. The blood he saw on the shattered windshield and on the steering wheel told him the driver had been injured. He realized that the truck engine had still been idling as it gave a last gasp and quit, the headlights dying with it.

Darkness fell over him with a bone-chilling silence. He listened for any sound, hearing nothing but his heartbeat. He pulled out his flashlight and shone it around the interior of the truck's cab.

He had no clue who'd been driving it or how badly they might have been injured. Not enough to knock them out even with all the blood present. The person had managed to get away. He told himself they had probably run off into the trees.

He walked around the front of the truck and found fresh footprints heading down toward the creek. He saw blood on one of the large stones above the water. Turning the flashlight farther down toward the creek, he saw no one.

Convinced the driver was gone, Dylan quickly made his way back up to the road and Cat. That he'd come so close to losing her tonight still had him shaken. She wasn't his, he told himself. But damned if she didn't feel like his. Was that because from the first time he saw her, he'd been intrigued by her?

Now it had gone far beyond simply being intrigued. He wanted her like he'd never wanted anything in his life. The worst part was that he wasn't sure he could have her. He wasn't sure she wasn't still grieving her husband the way everyone thought he was grieving his wife.

He topped the hill to the road and was relieved when he saw her assessing the damage to her patrol SUV and taking photos. She was again back in acting sheriff mode, trained for the job and leaning on that training for strength. He knew the feeling well. But he didn't doubt that she'd been shaken to her roots tonight. Nearly dying had to have brought the reality of what she might be involved in home.

He thought of the large truck at the bottom of the hillside smashed into the trees. That could have easily been Cat and her unborn baby in that crash. He shuddered to think of how tragically this night could have ended.

As it was, he'd done the one thing he'd tried so hard not to do. Get involved and put himself and his story back into the news. Once his name was picked up by the media, there would be a rehash of Ginny's death and of his brother's. There would be more speculation—especially if word got out that the prosecutor was reopening the case.

"I've already called DCI," she said. "They're sending a team now."

He nodded. "We need to pull off the road in case there is any more traffic tonight," he said as the reality of the situation settled over him.

"You saved my life and my daughter's," Cat said, meeting his gaze in the light of the vehicle's headlights. "Thank you, but what made you follow me?"

"Just a feeling," he said, realizing how deep he was in with this woman. "I had a feeling you needed me."

She smiled and he felt his heart lift even as he dreaded

what was to come. All the media attention again. Only this time worse, because this time Cat would be in the middle of it as well. No one realized how bad it could get until they were the focus of the media for weeks on end. Cat would soon know. But that might not even be the worst of it. Clearly she was now a target.

"I recognized the truck that forced me off the road and went after you," Dylan said. "It's one of mine from the ranch." He shook his head at her quizzical expression. "I have no idea who was driving it."

"Rowena?"

"If so, she put her head into the windshield and could be bleeding pretty badly right now."

"Why would she do this?" Cat said, voicing his own thoughts.

"She must think you're getting too close to the truth. Or maybe it's to show whoever she works for that she's doing something to keep us from finding the document before she can."

Chapter Seventeen

Dylan hadn't been able to sleep last night. He'd changed the passcode on the gate the moment he got back to find Rowena's car gone. He told himself it couldn't have been her driving his truck last night—unless she had help.

And that was what worried him.

According to Cat, the only time she saw Rowena away from the ranch was when she'd been talking to the man staying at the hotel. The man Cat thought was FBI. That man was now dead.

Who did that leave? Rowena, Patty Cooper Harper, Sharese and her brother Luca. Any of them could have been driving the truck. He knew Cat wanted to believe, as he did, that Patty had helped with his nephew's delivery and taken the infant to protect him. But then who had killed Athena? He hated to think that the woman who'd saved the baby would kill the mother. There was something so cold blooded about that... So even Patty could have been driving the truck since Rowena had access to it thanks to him letting her stay at the ranch.

He reminded himself that his own wife had been in on this and had gotten killed in a car bombing along with his brother. That was stone cold as well. These were apparently the kind of people he and Cat were dealing with. They could have both been killed last night. Whoever had been driving the old truck had certainly tried.

His fear was that the group couldn't find the document and without it, they were desperate because their lives were on the line. Desperate people made desperate decisions.

Dylan thought of Cat, his concern for her growing. She'd been taken off the case, put on desk duty. But that didn't mean she would be safe—even if she did her best to stay out of it. Knowing her, he doubted she would be able *not* to follow a lead if one presented itself.

That's why he had to keep her busy, he thought after hanging up from talking to the manager at the wrecking yard in Eureka. They had the truck. Forensics had finished with it. Dylan didn't hold much hope that they found any prints from last night's driver. But they could find his prints in the truck, possibly along with blood.

He'd really thought he had walked away from all of this. This morning he'd searched the cottage looking for the document. He'd assumed it would be on a thumb drive or something like it. But it could be old school and printed out on plain old paper. Either way, he had no luck finding it.

If Cat was right and Ginny had hidden it somewhere here on the ranch…why would she have done that? Once she had her hands on it, why not give it to her handlers? Unless she was trying to make a better deal. Is that where his brother came in? Beau had contacts around the world. He knew people. Had they been trying to sell it?

A thought struck him. What if she never had the list? What if Beau had contacted her with the list? Dylan didn't want to believe his brother had gone that bad, but right now he had more questions than answers. He feared he might never know the truth. That and worrying about Cat had kept him from sleeping last night. That he'd gotten this involved with her scared him. It had been so fast, so intense, more real than anything he'd ever experienced.

He picked up the phone, needing to see her. He didn't know if they could survive this as a couple, but somehow, he had to get the two of them out of it.

CAT KEPT THINKING about Athena Grant. Pregnant and running scared, the woman knew she was going to die, but Cat knew in her heart that she would have done whatever it took to save her baby—even call someone she knew she couldn't trust, someone who would kill her.

That was a love that Cat could understand better right now.

She'd gotten the call she'd been expecting first thing this morning. She was on desk duty for the rest of her time in Fortune Creek. She still had six weeks as acting sheriff and, while she had turned it over to DCI and the FBI, she didn't want to just walk away. She wanted to stop the people who had tried to kill both her and Dylan last night.

For her safety and that of her baby she'd needed to step back. Which meant she would stay to take calls at the office, sit in her chair and watch Helen knit and try to stay awake.

Her daughter kicked her, reminding her that she'd wished for something to happen to keep her awake and look how that had almost turned out. Well, she'd gotten more than she wished for. What had almost happened last night had shaken her to her core. It made her question if she could do this job even after she delivered her little girl. Could she risk her life knowing there was no one to take care of her daughter without her?

She saw Helen take a call, then look in her direction a moment before her phone rang. She picked up glad to hear Dylan's voice.

"I'm at the wrecking yard in Eureka. My pickup still runs. How about your patrol SUV?" It did. "Can I buy you lunch?"

"That sounds wonderful. Why don't I meet you there. I want to see the truck." Earlier she'd called the local hospitals to see if anyone had come in with a head injury. No one. If it had been Rowena, it was possible they would find her dead somewhere down in the trees along the creek. Unless her injuries weren't life threatening.

Dylan had called her last night to tell her that when he'd returned to the ranch after the two of them had given all their information to the DCI team and FBI, he'd found Rowena gone—just like his truck from one of the old barns. Everyone was anxious to talk to her.

Last night Cat had gotten only a glimpse of the truck just before it had gone off the road and disappeared. She was anxious to see it as she drove into town to the wrecking yard. Dylan was standing over by the truck when she got there. She parked, got out, and immediately felt off-balance at the sight of the big green truck with the wooden stock rack.

Even from a distance, she could see how the front was caved in from hitting a tree and putting the driver's head into the windshield. She had no idea what year it

was, what make or model, just that it was made before
seatbelts.

The closer she got to the truck, the more she felt the
tiny hairs on her neck stand on end. Cat couldn't believe what she was looking at. It was an old farm truck,
exactly as her husband described it to her and the cops
in the hospital before he died. The rusted door panel on
the driver's side. The faded green body but with a yel-
low hood that had apparently been replaced but never
painted to match. The metal-reinforced wooden stock
rack right down to the almost unreadable sticker on the
back of the large side mirror from a local café that was
no longer in business.

The truck was the one that had killed her husband.
Her heart threatened to burst from her chest. She looked
over at Dylan, the weight of it pressing on her chest.

"You're sure this is your truck?" Her voice sounded
odd even to her. She could feel Dylan next to her.

"It's mine. I found it in the barn when I bought the
place."

Cat felt sick. She didn't want to believe it, but this was
the truck. There couldn't be two of them exactly alike.
Not with that old café sticker on the back of the driver's
side mirror. Not with the metal added to the wooden
stock rack.

She stepped around the truck to look at the left-hand
side. The dent was there, along with the spot where the
paint had been scraped off, leaving the telltale white
paint from the vehicle her husband had been driving.
No wonder the truck hadn't been found after the accident. It had been in Dylan's barn.

This was the truck that had killed her husband.

"It's so old. It doesn't even look like it would run," she said, wondering what it was she wanted him to tell her—anything that could stop her thinking the worst.

"Surprisingly it still runs like a top."

"When was the last time you took it out for a drive?" she asked, her voice breaking. She could feel Dylan's intent gaze on her. He was standing so close that she could also feel the heat radiating off his body.

"I didn't know you had an interest in old farm trucks," he said, studying her. "It's been months since I even started it up."

Bile rose in her throat. She started to step away. "Cat?" Dylan reached for her arm to stop her. She let him since she felt as if she might crumble to her knees, her body felt so weak.

For months since she took the job, she'd been unconsciously looking for a truck just like it. But she hadn't seen one, not like this one. She'd thought she would never see the truck that hit her husband, that killed him, that left her pregnant and a widow.

Her gaze came up to Dylan's. "This is the truck that hit and killed my husband six months ago."

He stared at her, shock turning his handsome face into a pale mask of disbelief. "You said he was killed in a car wreck but—" He shook his head. "You can't think that I—" He let go of her to take a step back. "Cat, I swear I've never taken the truck off the ranch."

She felt tears burn her eyes. This is what she'd wanted to hear, wanted desperately to believe. She'd trusted this man. Trusted him with her body, her baby, her heart. "Then who?"

Dylan looked lost as he shook his head. "I don't know.

The key was in it when I discovered it in the barn. I never took it out. Someone could have stolen it, I guess, and…"

Cat shook her head, fear crushing her chest. "They wouldn't have brought it back. They couldn't have unless they knew the code to get back in the gate."

He looked sick. "When was your husband—" She told him the date and he let out a relieved breath. "I didn't come out to the ranch until three weeks after that. I remember the date. It was my birthday. Cat, I can prove I wasn't in Montana."

She stared at him still stunned and upset. "If it wasn't you, then…" She met his gaze and held it. "Didn't you say your wife was out here six months ago getting the house ready?"

He nodded slowly. "But why would Ginny take the truck out? What possible reason would she have?"

Cat looked at the truck with its huge wooden stock rack on the back. "Maybe she had to haul something." Like a body. Or furniture. Or load of machine parts she was taking to Canada to sell before bringing back drugs. Cat had no idea. "I'm going to have to get forensics to check out the bed of the truck as well as the cab, Dylan."

"Make the call. We need to know who was driving that truck not just last night but six months ago." As she started to pull out her phone, he stepped to her, pulling her into his arms and holding her. "I'm so sorry, Cat. So very sorry."

She nodded into his shoulder, thinking again of life's curves.

LEAVING THE TRUCK and the information with DCI, Dylan insisted on taking her to lunch. "I know you're not hungry, but maybe your daughter is."

She'd smiled at that. "I'm sorry I suspected you yet again," she said as they drove to a café.

He shrugged. "How could you not? All of this seems to have landed on my doorstep. No coincidence there. I'm tangled up in this every way but loose. My deceased wife, her friends, my brother." He shook his head as he parked. "I still can't fathom Ginny driving that truck the night your husband was killed. I married her, lived with her a short time. I realize now that she was a liar and probably a cheater, but to be so cold-blooded as to crash into your husband's car and not stop to help."

"I suppose it would depend on why she was driving the truck to begin with," Cat said after they'd gotten out and were walking toward the front door of the café. "I doubt she wanted anyone to know what she was doing out that night in the truck so close to the Canadian border. I'm just glad that Taylor was able to make a call for help or I wouldn't have gotten to say goodbye to him."

"Or learn about the truck that hit him," Dylan said as he opened the door, and they stepped inside.

Once seated, he said, "I'm so sorry. If I'd never married Ginny—"

She reached over and put a hand on his and shook her head. "This isn't your fault. No one can control fate."

He turned his hand over to take hers. "So true."

She looked lost in thought for a moment before she said, "Are you sure Ginny was out here alone?"

Frowning, he said, "You think Rowena or one of the others was with her?"

"I was thinking more like your brother."

He stared at her in surprise, realizing that he'd never questioned how long Ginny and Beau had been...what?

Conspiring or just simply having an affair behind his back? The waitress approached, took their orders and left before he dared speak or, worse, cuss.

"You think he was driving the truck that night?"

Cat seemed to wince. "No, I hadn't been thinking that, but if he was out here with her and they were hooked up in this scheme…"

"Scheming," he repeated. "Why not? He could have been driving. I'll see if I can find out if he was in the states during that time." He had no idea how long Ginny and his brother had been, as Cat put it, scheming. Or even if they had been. He made the call, quick and to the point, and disconnected.

"I'm sorry," she said as if it was a foregone conclusion that his brother had been in the states six months ago. He still held out hope that he was wrong.

"You have no reason to be sorry. I never cared what their story was." He laughed scornfully. "Probably because whatever it was would only make me feel worse."

"That's why I hate bringing it all back up."

"The investigation is bringing it back up. Rowena, Athena's death, her missing baby…" His gaze softened as he looked at her. "I've been hiding out here in Montana from the truth, but it's going to come anyway. It's time I faced it."

His cell rang and he quickly picked up. He listened for a few moments. He could feel her watching him, trying to see by his expression how bad it was. He wished he could hide his feelings better. He used to be good at it. He didn't want to be anymore. "Thank you. I appreciate this." He disconnected and looked at her.

"Beau was in the states. Want to bet he was in Montana?"

CAT ATE AS much of her salad as she could, the two of them having fallen silent as if both were lost in their own thoughts. "This doesn't mean Beau was driving the truck," she said after a while. "Nor does it mean he was on the wrong side of this. I'd like to take a look inside his lake house."

"No problem," he said after paying for their lunch and leading her outside to his pickup. "Want to pick up your SUV or go in the truck?"

"Let's take your truck."

They climbed in before he asked, "Anything special you're looking for?"

"Just a thought," she said. "Let's say Beau was trying to help Ginny get out rather than joining her. Let's say they weren't alone out here. Ginny didn't get the list from you. Maybe she wasn't the one to get it at all. Maybe she took it from Rowena, flew out here and met Beau asking for his help."

"That's a whole lot of supposition," he commented as he drove toward Flathead Lake.

"Then Ginny and Beau were killed in the bombing, but they didn't have the list with them." He nodded. "We know Rowena came out here looking for something. What if Beau and Ginny left it in his lake house so you would find it and take it to the right people."

"That really is a long shot," Dylan said, but she could tell he wanted to believe it. He wanted to believe in his brother—and maybe that there might have been something good in his deceased wife. "Then who was driving the truck not just last night but six months ago?"

She shrugged. "We have a lot of suspects. I'd put

Rowena at the top of the list, but I doubt she can drive a stick."

"Something tells me you can, Sheriff," he said grinning over at her.

"I'm a Montana girl. I can put my own worm on a hook, catch and gut a fish and fry it up for dinner."

He laughed. "My kind of woman." His look sent a bolt of heat right to her center. She felt her face flush as she thought of him between her legs. "So not Rowena," Dylan said.

"Let's not forget Sharese and her brother Luca."

"Or that Rowena visited Sharese in Libby before we were run off the road," he added.

"Just curious," Cat asked. "Did Ginny know how to drive a stick shift?"

DYLAN HAD NO IDEA. He couldn't believe how little he'd known about the woman he'd married. He also realized, as he pulled up to Beau's lake house, that Cat still thought Ginny might have been driving the truck six months ago.

The house felt colder than it had the last time they were there. He thought about how he'd brought Cat here wanting her desperately. That feeling hadn't gone away; he had a feeling it never would. There was something about her, her strength and yet her compassion that had him falling for her.

He reminded himself that he'd fallen this quickly for Ginny and look where that had left him.

"Did you know your brother was buying this place?" she asked as he snapped on the lights.

"Not until he'd already purchased it and invited me out."

They split up and began to search the house. It wasn't large, but it was nice. As he moved through it, seeing some of his brother's things, he hoped Cat was right and that his brother hadn't gone to the dark side.

But for the life of him, he couldn't imagine where his brother would have left the list. It made no sense that Beau was involved at all—unless he added in Ginny. Was Beau in love with her? Or was it a business deal? It would have been just like his brother to want to save the femme fatale in distress.

When he finished his part of the search, he found Cat back in the living room.

"If your brother got his hands on the document and realized what it was, why wouldn't he have just handed it over to you?"

Dylan shook his head. "We'd been at odds for a while before his death. I didn't like the way he was living. He didn't think I was doing such a great job of my life either." He shrugged. "Brothers, they disagree."

"But he was at your wedding."

"Apparently busy with Athena," Dylan said with a curse.

"Did he like Ginny?" she asked.

Dylan had to consider that. "He was wary. I got the impression he thought I jumped into it too quickly."

Cat nodded and looked around the room. "Did you spend any time here in this house with him?"

"I did when he first bought it." He saw that she'd walked to a shelf full of board games.

"Did you play any of these?"

He had to think. "Monopoly. Beau loved to make his

own money, refusing to touch his inheritance. So he especially liked to take every penny I had in the game."

"I think we should take a look at the game," Cat said. "We've looked everywhere else." She reached for it but was too short to take it off the shelf. Dylan stepped over to her, pulled down the game from the top shelf and took it over to the table.

"Is that where he normally kept the game?" she asked as she joined him.

He frowned. "I don't think I ever paid any attention." He lifted the lid and looked down at it, remembering their last game. He and Beau had fought tooth and nail, Dylan not about to let him win. "He always wanted the top hat," he said picking up the piece and turning it in his fingers.

"And you?" Cat asked sitting down before digging into the game box.

"I usually had the dog. Better than the wheelbarrow or the iron."

She chuckled at that. "I like the car." She picked up one stack of money and thumbed through it, then another, putting them aside.

Dylan took out the land titles and the Chance and Get Out of Jail Free cards. Nothing. He was ready to give up when Cat lifted the cardboard bottom up. He heard the sound she made. Her gaze shot to him as she moved the cardboard aside and he saw the envelope taped to the floor of the game box.

Chapter Eighteen

The sound of a boat motor grew louder. Dylan grabbed the envelope and started to open it when he realized the outboard motor had stopped. He quickly glanced out the window to see a boat pull in at Beau's dock. Two figures, one male, one female, were climbing out. The female secured the boat, the male had already started toward them.

"Let's go," he said putting the envelope into his jacket pocket and reaching for Cat. They hurried out the back door and into his pickup. He was backing out when he saw the male come around the corner of the house. He hit the gas as he whipped the pickup around and took off, losing sight of the man as they sped off.

"Did you recognize the man?" Cat asked.

"No, you?"

"Luca Harmon," Cat said as Dylan drove while watching his rearview mirror to see if they were followed. "Sharese's brother. I found a high school photo of him."

"I know what Fuller said about not destroying the document—if that's what's in this envelope, but I don't like having it in my possession." He glanced at her.

"Because it puts me in danger too," she said. "I am trained for this, you know."

"I know," he said and looked over at her again. "But I can't bear the thought of something happening to you and your baby."

He pulled out his phone to make the call. When the man answered, he said without preamble, "Fuller, I have it. How do I get it to you?" He listened to the directions the man gave him. "I'm on my way. I just have one stop to make."

"You trust Fuller?" Cat asked after he'd disconnected.

"I don't trust anyone." He looked over at her. "But you."

As DYLAN STARTED out of the wrecking yard, following Cat's patrol SUV, his cell rang. "Ike," he said, hoping his friend had some good news. "There seems to be a problem with the DNA found at the scene of the bombing. They can't find a match and some of the DNA has been misplaced."

"What does that mean? I was told that my brother and wife were in that car." He realized that while he'd seen Ginny get into the car, he'd never seen the driver. It was only later that he learned it had been Beau behind the wheel. "Are you telling me it wasn't my brother?"

"I'm telling you that they are running the DNA again. It was probably just a mix-up at the lab and that will be the end of it. I thought this would relieve your mind."

Dylan only wished it had. He found himself questioning everything. "Has anyone else that we know died recently?"

"You're asking about Allen Zimmerman."

"I am. If someone had a list of names and was coming after us…"

"It doesn't appear so," Ike said.

"I'm wondering who leaked the list." Dylan couldn't believe he was saying this.

"Not our own boss," his friend said. "I'll see what I can find out."

"Thanks." He hated to think he might be right. He had trusted Zimmerman with his life numerous times. But he also knew that people changed, circumstances changed.

He took out the envelope they'd found in the Monopoly game and opened it as he drove. Inside was a very slim thumb drive and a note in his brother's handwriting:

Be careful who you give this to.

That's all it said.

He put it back and followed Cat to Fortune Creek. Once he saw her safely into her office, he thought about going by the ranch to put the drive into his computer to see if the list was actually on it. But going near the ranch right now felt too dangerous. Only one person knew where he was going at this moment. Officer Fuller.

That thought made him suddenly uneasy.

Be careful who you give this to.

Dylan swore. He didn't know who to trust. But at least Cat should be safe back at her office. He told himself that this would all be over soon. But would they find his nephew?

He'd done his best not to think about the missing baby. It hurt too much to think that Beau had left something so precious, and Dylan might never get to see his nephew, let alone hold him.

He had to end this, but was giving the thumb drive to Fuller the right move?

He checked his rearview mirror to make sure he hadn't picked up a tail. Earlier he'd worried that he and Cat might be followed from the wrecking yard. They hadn't. It was hard to follow anyone on these narrow highways with so little traffic—unless you didn't mind being seen, he thought, remembering his big truck trying to force Cat off the road.

DYLAN HAD INSISTED on following Cat back to Fortune Creek. He now sat behind the wheel of his pickup parked in front of the sheriff's office determined to make sure she was safely inside. She waved as she pushed open the door and Helen looked up, pursed her lips and went back to her knitting.

Cat turned to see Dylan drive away, her heart in her throat. She hoped he was doing the right thing giving the information to Fuller.

"Any messages?" Cat asked.

"On your desk."

"Any chance the baby has been found?"

Helen looked up, her needles still going. "Probably would have mentioned that right away if he had been."

Maybe, Cat thought, not so sure about that. "And I would have appreciated it." She saw that Helen was now making something small out of pink yarn.

Turning away, she headed for her office. Dylan had the document. Once he handed it over and word was released that the list had been found and was back in safe keeping, this still wouldn't be over. It wouldn't be finished until Athena's and Beau's infant son was found.

In her office, Cat dropped into her chair. Her daughter had been kicking all day, especially when she'd recognized the truck that had hit Taylor. The statute of limitations on hit-and-run in Montana was three years. Whoever was driving that truck that night six months ago could still be arrested and convicted. Was it the same person who'd tried to run her off the road last night?

She went through her messages. Most were updates on the case. It had been Athena's blood in the passenger side seat of Patty Cooper's car. The baby had also been in the car. But there was no update on where Patty or the baby were now.

Same with Rowena. She too was missing.

Cat assumed Dylan would tell Fuller about Luca Harmon coming to the lake house as they were leaving with another individual, probably his sister Sharese.

According to the message from the DCI lab, DNA was taken from the truck windshield and steering wheel. No word on a match yet. There was a BOLO out on Rowena and Patty, but neither had been found. And Athena's baby was still missing. There had been numerous sightings of a woman with a baby, but none of them had turned up Patty Cooper and the missing baby boy.

Cat filed the messages, followed up on a few other things, cleaned her desk and noticed the time. The day was almost over. Helen was already packing up her things to go home and let dispatch in Eureka take over.

"You look tired," Helen said, appearing at Cat's office door. "You should go upstairs and get some rest."

Surprised at Helen's concern, Cat opened her mouth, but nothing came out. Before she could respond, the older woman turned and left, locking the front door behind her. She found herself smiling. That was the nicest Helen had been to her since she'd started this job. She was winning the woman over.

It was a small victory, but Cat would take it. She picked up her belongings and turned out the light as she headed for the back door and the stairs that would take her up to her apartment.

Her thoughts circled back to Dylan Walker, as they had since the day she'd met him. She'd let down her guard with him in a way that shocked her. She more than liked him, and she felt that he liked her as well. But they both had so much baggage. She cupped her protruding baby bump. Not to mention, the timing was definitely off. The last thing she wanted was Dylan to feel guilty for what had happened to Taylor and think he could make it right by…by what? Being with her?

What had happened the other day at the lake house, the way she'd surrendered to the passion, made her wonder. He'd done it for her pleasure, her satisfaction, she told herself as she climbed the stairs to her apartment. What about his own? He'd said another time, but another time hadn't presented itself. Because he thought their lovemaking had been a mistake?

Opening the apartment door, she reached in and flicked on the light. For a second, she was blinded by the sudden brightness. For a second, she didn't see the shape standing silhouetted against the front window. For a second, she didn't recognize the woman from the photographs she'd seen of her.

She did a double take, her voice cracking with both her fright and her shock as she said, "I thought you were dead."

Chapter Nineteen

Dylan called his friend Ike again. "I have some classified very sensitive data. I honestly don't know who to give it to. Can you find out what you can about a man named Brian Fuller. He spelled both names. He introduced himself as an officer with the regional CIA agency with a photo ID badge that would get him into the CIA office building. But my question is, can I trust him?"

"I'm going to have to get back to you."

Disconnecting, Dylan pulled off the main road and drove back into the hills to a spot where he could see the road behind him. It was empty. He waited, wondering how long before Fuller called. What he was really wondering was how anxious Fuller was to get his hands on this data. Too anxious might make Dylan suspicious.

The sun dipped behind the mountains, casting the landscape in shadow as clouds gathered and the temperature dropped. Spring in Montana, he thought. It was the ficklest of seasons, teasing with warm sunny days only to turn into winter in the snap of your fingers. He thought of his nephew and hoped he was someplace warm and safe. His thoughts turned to Cat only moments before she called.

"Hey, I was just thinking about you," he said without preamble when he picked up. Silence. He felt the hairs rise on the back of his neck, the cab of the pickup suddenly colder than just moments before. "Cat?" The word came out on a breath as his chest tightened and his heart began to pound harder.

"And I was hoping you were thinking about me," said his wife.

He gripped the phone. Some kind of DNA mix-up, wasn't that what Ike had said. He'd thought it had to do with Beau's DNA from the bombing. He thought of those few seconds when the car with his wife had been out of his sight. Enough seconds that she'd gotten out of the car before it blew? And what? Someone else had climbed in?

"Ginny?" He sounded calmer than he felt. His mind raced. This was no trick. It was definitely Ginny, and she was definitely calling from Cat's cell phone. "What's going on?"

Her laugh chilled him to his bones. "I was just visiting with your... Cat." She laughed again. "Really, Dylan?"

"Catherine Jameson is the acting sheriff there in Fortune Creek, Ginny."

"Yes, I'm aware of that. I'm also aware of your... relationship with the very pregnant acting sheriff. Not yours."

"I wish, but no. Didn't meet her until recently when she came out to the ranch suspecting me of murder. But you wouldn't know anything about that, right? Because you've been playing dead."

"You sound bitter. I had really hoped that you had found happiness out here in the sticks and were getting over me."

"Let me talk to Cat."

"She's busy."

He ground his teeth. His hand gripped the phone so hard it ached. "Ginny, I was hoping that it would turn out that you were one of the good ones, double-crossing your bad friends to do the right thing and that's what had gotten you killed."

"You never understood me, Dylan."

"But I'm definitely beginning to."

"Good, since we should meet. I'll bring your little sheriff along for the ride. Come to the ranch, oh and, lover…? Be sure to bring the thumb drive. Make sure it is just you, no feds; otherwise, it would be awful if anything happened to your… Cat."

With that, she disconnected. Dylan swore. Ginny was alive. Why wasn't he more surprised? Because the woman was a liar, a spy, a killer since she'd let some other woman die to cover her tracks. Some relative of hers since the DNA had been a close-enough match that it hadn't been caught the first time around?

He took a breath, let it out and tried to calm down. He couldn't underestimate what Ginny might do, especially to Cat. Rowena must have told her about him and the acting sheriff. He'd only managed to put Cat in more danger, but now he had to play this carefully, he told himself, as he started his pickup and drove toward the ranch.

He made only one call. "Ike, Ginny is alive and has taken the acting sheriff from Fortune Creek, who is seven months pregnant. I'm headed to the ranch. Let the FBI know—but tell them not to move in until I give them a signal."

"A signal."

"They'll know if they are close to the ranch," he said. "Good luck."

IT DIDN'T TAKE a lot of persuading to get Cat into the van that pulled up behind the sheriff's department. She recognized the driver from earlier today when he'd come racing up in a boat. Luca Harmon drove while Cat rode in the back with his sister Sharese. Cat recognized her from her Montana driver's license photo. Like Cat, Sharese didn't look happy to be there, especially with Ginny holding a gun on them both.

"So how did it work?" Cat asked Ginny. "You got in the car but didn't go far before you got out and someone else got in before the car blew up? Or did Dylan just think he saw you get into the car? Someone in the same dress, about the same height, same hairdo?"

Ginny mugged a face. "What does it matter? I'm alive and here."

"Anyone we know?" Sharese asked, sarcastically. "Or just someone you chose off the street to die in your place?" Ginny ignored her.

"But where did Beau Walker fit in?" Cat asked.

This got a smile out of Ginny. "He was very helpful."

"And apparently paid a high price for it," the sheriff said. "Unless he got out of the car too."

Ginny shook her head. "Some people have to die for the cause."

"Just not you," Sharese said, seeming not bothered as the gun moved to point more in her direction than Cat's.

"When's your baby due?" Ginny asked.

"Six weeks or so," she answered, thinking it was probably obvious anyway. "What about Rowena? I'm assuming like Athena, she's dispensable," Cat said. "What about Athena's baby though?"

Ginny shook her head and called up front to Luca. "Are we about there yet? I'm really getting tired of being interrogated back here."

"Rowena is a foot soldier," Sharese said. "She just isn't smart enough to know what happens to the foot soldiers when they are no longer needed. Like Athena."

"Athena turned on us," Ginny snapped. "She knew the price of betrayal."

"Did her baby know that price too?" Cat asked and grimaced, her hand going to her stomach. She saw Ginny's eyes widen just as she'd hoped.

"Where is the baby?" Sharese asked. "If I find out you killed—"

Dylan's not-so-dead wife gave her cohort a warning look. "We aren't monsters. We're no different from people in this country. We just have our own beliefs and see the world order differently."

Cat kept pretending to have contractions. She could see Ginny's worried look since another baby wasn't part of her plan. "Were you driving the truck that night six months ago when you killed my husband or was Luca?"

The question caught Ginny completely off guard. It was the first time Cat had seen the gun in her hand waver. Not that she was about to try to disarm Ginny in this van. They were on their way to the ranch. All she could hope was that she would get a chance once there.

"I don't know what—"

"Sure you do," Cat continued, holding her hand over her stomach and wincing. "You'd taken that big old farm truck out of the barn and driven up to the border probably carrying some form of contraband when you hit a white car my husband was driving on his way home from a fishing trip. He lived long enough to give a description of the truck—just not the driver."

"That was him?" Luca asked, turning from the driver's seat. "I told you to slow down."

"Shut up," Ginny snapped at him, her gaze locked with Cat's.

"So it was you," Cat said. "Once I saw the truck I had a feeling you were driving it that night."

"She's known for her reckless behavior," Sharese said. "Always just looking out for number one."

"You really should shut up too, Sharese," Ginny ground out from between clenched teeth even as her gaze remained locked with Cat's. "That was your husband?" She motioned her head toward Cat's baby bump.

Cat spoke as if in physical pain. "I never got to tell him I was pregnant."

Ginny looked uncomfortable and concerned now. "I always wanted a baby."

"That's not what Dylan says," Cat said.

She shrugged. "There's a lot Dylan doesn't know about me, but it seems he knows you fairly well and in such a short time. He apparently didn't learn anything about falling in love too quickly with me."

"It wasn't love with you," Sharese said. "It was the package you presented with that whole body of yours and the lies you told him. He didn't see the ugly self-centered rotten insides of you."

The tension in the van kicked up a few more notches. Cat half expected Ginny to shoot the woman.

"I do what I do for the cause," Ginny snapped.

Sharese scoffed. "You don't care about the cause. You jumped on board because it gave you an excuse to hurt people in the name of some ideal that I doubt you even understand."

"Enough," Luca called back to his sister as the van slowed and he made the turn into the ranch.

The air felt heavy and dark as they bumped along the road to the gate. Cat wondered if Dylan was already here. He'd said that he'd changed the code. Even Rowena shouldn't have been able to get in.

But as they approached the gate, Cat saw that it was standing open. The sight gave her little hope of how this was going to end.

DYLAN STOOD ON the deck of his cottage waiting. Ginny had Cat. He could feel the thumb drive in his jeans' pocket. His phone was in his other pocket, ready to send in the troops.

His weapon was tucked into the back of his jeans, covered by his shirt. But it wasn't the only one on him. He feared if it came down to gunplay, they would all lose. But at the same time, he knew he'd do whatever he had to so Cat and her unborn baby left here alive.

In the distance he saw a van come roaring out of the trees headed for him. He fisted his hands at his sides for a moment, then tried to relax. He had no idea how many people were in the van or what Ginny would do once she had the thumb drive. Three of her associates were dead—probably killed by friendly fire.

Did she plan on getting rid of everyone who knew about the thumb drive? That led him to believe that she didn't plan to turn it over to either the US or Russia. She must have put it up for auction, betraying not just her native country and her adopted country, but those comrades she'd pulled into her scheme.

The van stopped just feet from the deck. Still, he waited. Ginny was in control—at least for the moment.

The side door on the van rolled open loudly a few moments before Ginny stepped out. If she was scared, she didn't look it. She didn't look all that much different from the last time he'd seen her. Except now she wore canvas pants, a T-shirt and combat boots and held a gun in her hand.

She smiled at him for an instant before she pulled Cat out of the van, using her as a shield. He saw the gun leveled at the acting sheriff's back.

For a moment, no one moved, then the driver of the van killed the engine and climbed out. Luca Harmon. Ginny said something to whoever was still in the van and a moment later a woman he recognized from the salon photo stepped out. Sharese Harmon.

Everyone seemed to be waiting for Ginny's orders.

"You know what I'm here for," his not-so-deceased wife said. "Give it to me or I will kill your...Cat."

"That was cute the first time, Ginny, but now it's getting a little stale. I want to know where my nephew is."

She eyed him, seeming surprised that he didn't look scared or worried or even anxious. She glanced around as if realizing she might have walked into a trap. The spring day had turned into a cloudy, cold evening with the sky spitting ice crystals that hung in the twilight. Any moment it would start to snow.

"Why don't we take this inside where it's warmer?"

he said and started to turn toward the cottage. Out of the corner of his eye he saw Sharese and her brother start toward the deck steps and stop abruptly as Ginny spoke.

"This isn't that kind of visit," she barked. "Give me what I came here for and then we'll leave."

"You won't be leaving with Cat."

Ginny chuckled at that.

"I'm still waiting. Where is my nephew?" he demanded.

She shook her head. "I don't know why you're stalling but it's making me nervous. I hope I don't pull the trigger accidently and kill your girlfriend. The thumb drive, Dylan. *Now!*"

Chapter Twenty

Cat wondered if Dylan believed Ginny was going to let any of them go once she had the drive. Cat didn't think so, but she also didn't want to take the chance that the woman might shoot them all if she didn't get what she wanted.

As far as Cat could tell, Luca wasn't armed. Sharese either. But the hairdresser was feisty enough that she could have a weapon on her. Cat would assume that Ginny would have checked before, when Sharese and her brother had picked her up in the van and then dropped her off at the sheriff's office apartment.

Clearly Ginny didn't trust anyone, even her own cohorts. Cat met Dylan's gaze and held it. She hoped she was reading it correctly as she winked, then suddenly grabbed her stomach, let out a cry of pain and bent over as if having a major contraction. The sound of a gunshot echoed around her, terrifying her that Ginny had pulled the trigger on the gun that had been pressed to her back. She realized that the woman was wounded as Ginny grabbed her by the hair and began to pull her toward the open van door, using Cat as a shield.

But the sheriff made herself into dead weight, slumping forward and slowing their progress. Ginny was yelling for Luca and Sharese to help her. Out of the corner of her eye, Cat saw Dylan launch himself off the deck at Ginny.

What she hadn't seen was Luca. He came flying toward them, intercepting Dylan. Sharese rushed to get behind the wheel of the van and now started it up.

Ginny almost had the two of them to the van door. Cat knew that she couldn't let Ginny force her back into the van. She and her baby were as good as dead if she did. She kicked back at the woman, bringing her boots down on Ginny's ankle. She heard her cry out in pain and jerk hard on the handful of Cat's hair in her fist, forcing her toward the gaping door of the van.

DYLAN DOVE OFF the deck. There was no way he was going to let Ginny take Cat. He almost had his hands on Ginny when Luca charged him from the side, driving them both to the ground. They grappled on the ground, Luca clearly trained for combat. Dylan hadn't had to use his training in a long while. He wished he could say the same for Luca as they fought.

At the same time, he tried to keep an eye on Cat and Ginny. He saw her stomp on Ginny's ankle, then hit her hard in the side with an elbow. Heard the cry of pain she made as Cat swung around going for the gun. He fought harder, terrified for Cat and her baby as he watched the sheriff try to wrestle the gun away from Ginny.

Cat shoved Ginny hard, slamming her into the side of the van, both still fighting for the gun. Ginny still had a death grip on the weapon. She had height and weight against Cat, but the sheriff was holding her own.

As he and Luca fought, Dylan heard Sharese rev the van's engine. She was yelling for Luca to get in when the gun Cat and Ginny had been fighting over went off. A few seconds later, the van lurched and died, rolling slowly backward. The horn began to honk as Sharese slumped over the wheel.

Luca cried out and struck Dylan, catching him in the jaw and knocking him backward before racing to his sister. Dylan righted himself and launched himself at Ginny. She'd been momentarily distracted as she and Cat were forced back from the moving vehicle.

He quickly wrestled the gun away and turned the weapon on her. "Move and I will shoot you."

Ginny stumbled back, blue eyes glittering with malice as he pulled Cat to him. He could see that she was breathing hard but didn't seem the worse for wear. Still he asked, "Are you all right?"

"Fine," Ginny snapped.

"I was talking to Cat."

"Fine," Cat said, but he saw her hand go to her stomach as if she was worried about her baby.

Cat could hear the worry in Dylan's voice, see it in his expression as the FBI came charging out of the trees. It took little time after that to take Luca and Ginny into custody.

By then, she was in Dylan's arms, the baby between them, both with a hand on her stomach. She waited to feel her daughter kick. Time seemed to stretch out forever before she felt her daughter moving again. Tears welled in her eyes as she nodded. She was all right. Her baby was all right.

But Dylan insisted a helicopter be ordered to take Cat to the hospital to make sure she was all right. He led her over to the deck, insisted she sit as they both gave their statements to one of the agents. His concern comforted her. There was no doubt in her mind that Ginny would have killed them all.

Both Ginny and Luca were now in cuffs in the back of a large SUV as the agents searched for anyone else who might have been involved. Still no sign of Rowena or Patty or the baby. The coroner had been called for Sharese. Agents had had to pull Luca away from his deceased sister. Even now, he was still beside himself, head down, silently sobbing.

Dylan asked to speak to Ginny and Luca before they were taken away. He stood at the open window looking in at Ginny and Luca. Cat heard most of the conversation, her heart breaking for him. "I used to think you were beautiful," he said to his wife. "I no longer do. There is something so cold and cruel in you, so soulless. I don't understand how you could have hurt so many people. Please, Ginny, at least tell me where I can find my nephew."

Ginny stared at him for a moment before smiling. "You'll never have him. He's ours now."

He shook his head. Cat could see that he was fighting the urge to choke the truth out of the woman. Cat felt the same way. It shocked her the animosity she felt. It made her question her time as acting sheriff.

Luca's head came up, his eyes puffy from crying, his face blotchy. "Patty has your nephew," he said between sobs.

"Shut up!" Ginny snapped. "If you say another word—"

Luca spat out the words. "*You killed my sister.*"

"It was an accident, you fool."

Luca shook his head. "My sister and I didn't want any of this and you knew it. You dragged us into this." He turned to one of the FBI agents right outside the vehicle. "I'll tell you everything."

"Where can I find Patty?" Dylan asked and Luca gave him an address.

One of the FBI agents said, "We're on it."

"What about Rowena?" Dylan asked Luca, who only shook his head before he said, "Gone."

"Dead?"

Luca shrugged and looked at Ginny. "Probably."

Agents were headed for the address Luca had given them. Cat breathed a sigh of relief, smiling as Dylan put his arm around her and they headed to the chopper now setting down some distance away.

His look said that he'd found out what he could, now all he cared about was making sure Cat and her baby were all right.

After the FBI had arrived, everything had been a blur of activity. Cat told herself that her daughter was fine as they climbed into the chopper. Her baby was kicking maybe more than usual, but other than that…

Feeling exhausted, she closed her eyes as Dylan took her hand and squeezed it gently as if to say everything was going to be all right. She tried to think positive thoughts. Dylan told her that the FBI was going to pick up Patty Cooper Harper and his nephew at the address Luca had given them.

She thought of JP. The coroner had come over to her before he'd left with Sharese's body. He'd said he wanted to be sure she was all right, then given her a thumbs-up before leaving. She was beginning to think of him as a grandfather figure, cranky and yet cool in that he knew interesting stuff. Maybe she was injured, she thought, given the trail her mind had taken.

As much as Cat wanted to tell herself it was over, she knew she couldn't until the doctor told her that her baby was fine. Until Dylan had his nephew in his arms. She couldn't believe the way her boring job had turned out, as she and Dylan were strapped in and the chopper rose up above the trees headed for the hospital in Kalispell.

Once there, Dylan didn't leave her side until the doctor assured her that her daughter was fine. By then, it was morning. "But no more cops and robbers," he said. "Take it easy these last few weeks."

Cat smiled, nodding in relief. She would take it easy, she told herself as Dylan called the chopper to take her back to the ranch.

"He's going to pick us up out back. Ready?"

She hugged her stomach, feeling her daughter trying to get comfortable in the small space. They were both anxious for the infant to come bursting out into the world. Cat couldn't wait to meet her.

When she looked over at Dylan he was watching her, a frown on his face.

"I'm fine," she tried to reassure him.

"I know."

"That's not what's bothering you," she said. "Did they find Patty and the baby?"

He shook his head. "When they got to the address, she'd already left. They found lots of baby clothing and supplies. Apparently Patty is taking good care of him.

They'll find her. They have to. The last person who saw them said that she had the baby and was so loving toward him that they'd thought she must be the mother."

"The feds will find him," she said, touching Dylan's arm. She'd been so relieved that her daughter was all right that she'd just assumed the call had been from the FBI and they'd found Patty and the baby.

Nothing was over for Dylan. His deceased wife had come back and was now headed for jail, but he still didn't know the part his brother Beau had played in all this. Of course, it wasn't over for him and wouldn't be until he had his nephew.

THE CHOPPER LANDED in the same spot it had earlier at the ranch. The van Sharese had been killed in was gone and so was any evidence of what had happened there last night.

Still Dylan felt a chill as he and Cat disembarked and headed for his pickup parked in front of the cottage. Nothing looked amiss, yet he found himself searching for movement, his senses all on alert. He saw that there was a light on in the big house upstairs. Rowena must have left it on.

Cat must have followed his glance because she picked up on his unease. She slowed and moved closer to him. The spring breeze had a bite to it he recognized. Snow. He breathed in the cold, almost welcoming it. They were almost to his pickup when he heard a baby cry.

The startling sound made him freeze, Cat next to him. "I want you to get into my pickup and leave," he whispered as he fished out his truck keys and handed them to her.

She took the keys, but said, "I'm not leaving you."

"Cat," he said impatiently. "Think of your baby."

"I'm thinking of mine and yours." They heard the sound again and both looked toward the cottage. Cat started moving toward the deck. Neither was armed. The feds had taken Dylan's weapons as well as Cat's.

He touched her arm. "Let me get my gun out of the pickup." He moved swiftly to the truck. It was unlocked. He reached in, felt under the seat and knew at once that the gun was gone. No reason to check the glove box. There wouldn't be a small one in there either.

Closing the pickup door, he stepped back and noticed the odd way the truck was sitting. A glance under it solved that mystery. His right front tire was flat. He no longer thought Cat could get away. They were on their own here.

Cat seemed to notice his expression and looked again to the cottage where the baby had begun to cry louder. He knew there was no stopping her. She moved in that direction again, Dylan at her heels. She reached the door and opened it, but he insisted on going in first, determined to protect her to the end.

Once inside, he stopped to listen. It was dark except for a faint light toward the back of the cottage. He waited for his eyes to adjust. The crying was coming from a bedroom at the back. Seeing no motion, he stepped into the kitchen, drew out a knife from the rack, then followed the sound, afraid of what he would find. Cat was right behind him—after taking a small cast-iron skillet from where it hung next to the stove. It would have been comical, the two of them moving down the hall, if it hadn't been so serious.

The bedroom door was open, light spilling out along with the sound of the crying baby. Reaching the doorway, Dylan hesitated. He told himself it could be a recording to lure them down here. He thought he was right when the crying stopped.

He peered around the edge of the doorway and quickly jerked back, shocked at what he saw.

CAT HAD NO idea what Dylan had seen, but whatever it was had spooked him.

"You can come in," said a weak female voice from inside the bedroom. "I won't hurt you."

Something about the voice sent a chill through Cat. She pushed past Dylan into the doorway and stopped dead. The woman sitting in the chair by the window holding the baby looked like a ghost. Her skin was deathly pale, and a large bump protruded from her forehead. Both her eyes were blackened, her nose sat at an odd angle, and smears of dried blood covered her cracked upper lip.

Cat felt shock ricochet through her. She glanced at the baby, fearing it too had been injured. It didn't appear the infant was hurt, even as he began to cry again. Patty Cooper Harper looked nothing like her photo, but Cat knew it was her. She edged to the woman's chair, setting the small cast-iron skillet aside.

"May I hold him?" she asked, her voice cracking. For a moment she didn't think the woman would release him. The baby was wrapped in a small blanket that was stained with blood.

Patty looked down at the baby, a painful smile on her face as she slowly held him out to Cat.

The instant he was in her arms, Cat moved to the bed

and laid him down so she could open the blanket and make sure it wasn't his blood. Her heart was pounding with fear. They finally had the missing baby. *Please don't let him be injured.*

Dylan snapped on the overhead light as she peeled back the blanket and inspected the infant. He appeared unharmed. He looked up at her then began to cry again. "I need a couple of towels," Cat said, trying to keep her voice calm.

Dylan produced several large ones. She placed the baby in one, then wrapped him up in a second one, before she began to rock him. The infant quieted in a few moments.

"Has he been fed?" she asked Patty, who nodded.

"I took care of him," she said quietly. Her eyes looked dark, hollow.

"Who hurt you?" Cat asked as Dylan went to the woman. Patty didn't answer, her eyes on Dylan.

"She's going to come back and kill us all." Tears formed in the woman's eyes and ran unheeded down her cheeks. "The baby too. I tried to fight her off but she..." Patty seemed unable to finish.

"How badly are you hurt?"

"Too bad." She looked to Cat holding the baby, rocking him in her arms. "Don't let her hurt him." Her eyes seemed to widen as if she'd heard the same thing Cat had. Someone had just opened the front door. Patty began to cry silently with sobs that racked her body.

DYLAN HAD HEARD the cottage door open as well. He looked at Cat, a silent message passing between them as she held the baby closer. He hid the knife up the sleeve of his shirt and moved to the door. There was so much he needed to say to her, desperately wanted to say. He just hoped he got the chance.

He could hear someone in the kitchen moving around. Stealthily, he closed the bedroom door and crept down the hallway, unsure who or what he would find. When he'd first bought the house, the Realtor had warned him about bears making themselves at home if he left a window or door unlocked.

But he knew it wasn't a black bear in his kitchen. As he reached the kitchen opening, he started to glance in when he heard Rowena's annoying voice.

"No reason to be sneaking around," she said as she turned from the sink where she'd been washing her hands. She dried them on her bloody pants. He caught the smell of smoke on her as one hand went into her pocket and came back out with one of his guns. She didn't point it at him. Instead, she held it at her side, almost daring him to make a move.

"Can't wait to hear what you've been up to," he said, not bothering to hide his disgust for the woman.

"Just finishing up here at the ranch," she said. "Make a girl a drink?"

His first instinct was to tell her to go to hell, but he curbed it and moved cautiously toward the living room. At the bar, he called back to her, "There's no ice in the bucket."

"I'll rough it this one time and go without," she said.

He didn't think she would shoot him before she had the drink as he slipped the knife from his sleeve and hid it next to the ice bucket. He worried that she was too smart and too well trained to let him get close enough to use the knife anyway. She had his guns from the pickup. He'd bet she'd also searched the house for more. She knew she had the upper hand and that he and Cat and the baby and Patty were now at her mercy.

"It's over, Rowena," he said as he mixed up the gin and tonic she liked. "Ginny and Luca are in jail. Sharese is dead."

"No loss there," the woman said, suddenly closer than he'd realized. He could barely smell her perfume under the stench of smoke. She just wasn't close enough to keep her from shooting him before he could disarm her or stop her with the knife.

He could hear in her voice how she was enjoying being one of the few left standing. Was she now in charge? It would appear so. The power had already gone to her head. This is probably what she'd always wanted. He thought about her relationship with Ginny. Rowena must have been jealous as hell, resenting his wife, wanting what she had. Did that include him? He thought Cat might have been right about hoping to seduce him. Like that was ever going to happen, he thought.

He took his time finishing her drink with a slice of lime from the small container. Rowena would have preferred a fresh cut wedge, but then again, he doubted she would have wanted him using a knife.

Catching a glow through the nearby window, he looked in the direction of the big house on the side of the hill. It wasn't caused by the small light upstairs he'd seen earlier. This light was much brighter and appeared to be growing brighter by the moment. He realized what it was and let out a small laugh as he turned slowly to hand her the drink.

"You burned down my house?" he asked laughing. "The house I hated and refused to live in?"

"It was a symbolic gesture," she said, sounding angry. "Put the drink down there." She pointed to a side table. He did as she asked and moved again to the bar where there was at least one weapon at his disposal.

As she took the drink in her free hand and stepped back out of his range of attack, he noticed how tired she looked. "You look exhausted. Burning down houses isn't as easy as you thought, huh?"

Her gaze locked with his as she took a sip of the drink, and he saw fury in those blue eyes. He noticed that the gun was no longer at her side. It was now pointed at his heart.

"Mind if I make myself a drink?" he asked, already turning back to the bar and the knife. "I didn't expect you to come back here, figured you got whatever you'd come here for and were long gone."

"You know that's not true," she said with a chuckle. "You made sure I didn't get what I came here for." Again he heard something in her voice, a need for revenge against the woman she'd called her best friend—and that woman's husband.

"Can't imagine why you'd come back, especially just to burn down my house," he said as he poured a drink and considered both the knife and the heavy silver ice bucket partially filled with melted ice.

"Ginny thought she was so smart marrying you," Rowena said. "She was fulfilling her mission and then she was free—as long as she came through with the goods—the names of the US undercover operatives in the Soviet

Union who'd been responsible for the deflection of the country's famous ballet star Giselle."

"This is about a ballet dancer?" Dylan demanded, half turning to look back at her. He'd never understand Russian politics.

"She was our leader's favorite," Rowena said.

"Of course," he mocked. "So, what went wrong?"

"Ginny." Her gaze hardened. "She started falling in love with you and wanted out."

He turned back to his drink. This wasn't what he wanted to hear. He'd faced the woman only hours ago. That hadn't been love in her eyes. "I don't believe you."

"She couldn't go to you, so she got your brother to help her. She was going to sell us out for you."

He shook his head, his hands fisting at his sides. "She got my brother killed."

"He knew what he was getting into," Rowena said flippantly.

He finished making his drink and picked up the glass, squeezing so hard he feared it would break. Every cell of him wanted to stop this woman, finish this and get Cat and his nephew to safety.

But Rowena wanted him to try to get the jump on her. He could feel her waiting, sipping her drink, probably even smiling to herself. He knew she could shoot him before he could spin around. He took a sip of his drink and carefully put it down. As he did, he took hold of the edge of the ice bucket telling himself that if he flung it at her before he attacked, he might stand a chance.

"I hope I'm not interrupting anything," Cat said from behind them.

He froze, his hand loosening on the ice bucket as he

slowly, carefully turned to see her standing a few yards behind Rowena. She was holding the baby wrapped in the towels he'd gotten for her, her expression fierce. She'd never looked more beautiful, he thought with a jolt that rocketed through him.

In those seconds, Rowena spun around, leading with the gun. Dylan's heart leapt to this throat as he rushed her. He expected to hear the sound of a gunshot. Instead, he heard a surprised cry from Rowena. Past her, he saw that Cat had thrown the baby at her. Rowena had dropped her drink and raised her arms either to protect herself or the baby—only to see the towels uncoiling as they flew through the air revealing nothing inside.

Taking advantage of Rowena's surprise, Dylan grabbed her from behind and twisted the gun from her fingers. She fought, screaming and crying as he took her to the floor.

"Ginny made me do it," she cried. "I had no choice. It was all her idea. She told me to find the thumb drive, then make you pay."

"It doesn't matter, Rowena," Dylan told her. "It's over. We know that the only reason you came out here in the first place was to find the missing document. You failed."

"That wasn't the only reason." Her gaze was pleading. "I was as pretty as Ginny, smarter, and I had money. I still have money."

He shook his head as he heard what she was asking. "I'm sorry, but you're not my type."

Rowena jerked angrily under him. "And she is?" she demanded, motioning her head toward Cat.

"She is," he said nodding.

"You are so going to pay," Rowena spat out, the words

hard and cold. "Your brother double-crossed us and look what happened to him. Now it's your turn."

"Beau paid with his life, Rowena. Wasn't that enough?"

She shook her head angrily as her gaze shot to Cat. "I wish you'd died the other night on the road. You're the one who should have crashed into the trees!" Her gaze swung back to Dylan. "I knew how to get to you. Take out your girlfriend."

"You were driving the truck?" he demanded through clenched teeth.

"Not me. I can't drive a stick shift," Rowena said. "Patty. But she failed and I got stuck babysitting that brat of Athena's. You should be thanking me. If Ginny had gotten her hands on that baby…"

At the sound of the baby crying down the hall, Cat hurried to retrieve him. When she returned, he saw from her expression that Patty was also gone. She cuddled the infant to her, the crying stopping as the sound of sirens filled the air.

"Patty's gone," Cat said to Rowena. "Everyone is either in jail or dead."

Rowena snorted. "You're the ones who killed Patty, the two of you, running her off the road. When she hit that tree, the steering wheel crushed something inside her. She hasn't been the same since. I'm surprised she survived this long."

"Why didn't you get her to a doctor?" Cat cried, only to have Rowena give her an impatient look.

"Why do you think?"

"Well, it's over now," Dylan said.

Rowena glared at him. "You think this is over? It will never be over. There's more of us, lots more of us."

"And more of us," Cat said. "You're fighting a losing battle."

As Dylan let the federal officers take Rowena away, he reached for Cat, drawing her to him. After a moment, she said, "Would you like to hold your nephew?"

He felt his eyes burn with hot tears. Beau's son. He'd feared that he would never get to see him—let alone hold him. His throat constricted as he nodded, and she put the infant in his arms. He was almost afraid he would break down when he looked into the infant's tiny precious face.

What was he going to do with a baby? But then he did look. He felt a jolt. Baby Doe was the spitting image of Beau when he was a baby. He felt his heart fill and he knew. They were both going to be all right. Wasn't this what he'd always wanted, a family? He just hadn't dreamed of becoming a family like this. But he could do this, he could raise this baby on his own. It was what his brother would have wanted. It was also what he suspected Athena had wanted when she'd tried to reach him.

He glanced up at Cat and smiled through his tears. She too was crying. Peering down again at the beautiful baby in his arms, he whispered, "You're safe now. We're going to be just fine, you and me. You'll see."

Chapter Twenty-One

A strange quiet filled the days after the last of the arrests, Cat thought. It was spring in Montana, the sunny afternoons causing everything around Fortune Creek to turn green. The air smelled of new growth as grass emerged and trees sprouted leaves. The sky even seemed bigger and bluer with each day.

Cat had returned to the office and Helen. Dylan had done what he could for his nephew, who'd been sent by the court into foster care until the paperwork was completed and he could petition for guardianship and eventually adoption.

Then he'd been forced to go back to Washington, DC, to iron out things in the investigation. Cat knew that he personally wanted to give the list to someone he trusted. She wondered where the list of operatives had come from. She assumed that someone had gotten it to Ginny in the first place. She hoped Beau hadn't been in a position that he had access to the list and had foolishly been the one to give it to her, believing she was on the side of good.

But at some point, Beau had learned the truth and hidden the thumb drive in the game he and Dylan liked to play with a note to be careful who he trusted. That told her Beau was trying to do the right thing and that was what had gotten him killed.

She wanted Beau's name cleared not just for Dylan but for his son. The man she'd come to care for had enough betrayal in his life. Dylan didn't need more. He called every night. She knew he was excited to get back to the ranch. He was anxious to finally have his nephew under his roof. Cat couldn't be happier for him, knowing he was going to make a great father. That was what he would eventually become, not an uncle, but a father after the adoption.

She knew how anxious he was for that. She certainly could understand the feeling. She knew nothing about becoming a mother. But like Dylan, she was excited and ready for whatever it brought. Her daughter seemed to be anxious to make her exit. Cat felt as if she might burst with the life growing inside her.

Meanwhile, she had her own case to finalize. She spent a few days writing up her report. Cat was glad when they got word from Sheriff Parker that he and his bride Molly were returning to town. Molly was anxious to start her store in one of the old empty buildings in town, Cat heard. She hadn't spoken with the sheriff, nor had she met him. He'd already taken off on his honeymoon when she'd been assigned the job. After everything that had happened, he'd decided it was time to bring his wife home.

Cat had been looking forward to meeting this legend in Fortune Creek almost as much as Helen was looking forward to his return. They had both been waiting expectantly when he and Molly walked into the office.

Helen had let out a shriek and dropped her knitting

to race over to him. For a moment, Cat thought she was going to throw her arms around the man. But Helen stopped short and said, "Nice to have you back, Sheriff." Then her gaze had taken in Molly, the pretty, dark-haired woman by his side. "You too," Helen said with less warmth.

Molly smiled and said, "Good to see you again, Helen."

By then the sheriff had spotted Cat in his office. "Sheriff," she said, seeing why he was so popular. He was handsome and had a great smile. She awkwardly stood.

"Heard you had your share of trouble, Sheriff."

She couldn't help smiling. "Nothing Helen and I couldn't handle."

He grinned at that. "I can well imagine." He motioned her back into her chair. "I'm just stopping by since I'm not officially back for another few days. Just wanted to introduce myself to the famous Sheriff Cat Jameson."

"Acting Sheriff Cat Jameson," she said, touched by his kind words. "And I believe you mean infamous."

He shook his head. "My hat's off to you," he said as he touched the brim of his Stetson. "It's a pleasure to meet you." He stepped toward her, extending his hand. "Congratulations, Sheriff," he said, his grip strong and warm. "For a job well done."

Cat chuckled. "Thanks, but it's nice to have you back."

She heard Molly telling Helen about the house Brandt was having built for them. Apparently, they wouldn't be staying in the tiny apartment upstairs.

"In the meantime, we'll be staying at the hotel," Brandt told Cat. "You're welcome to stay upstairs as long as you like."

"I'm not sure of my plans," she said, her hands going to her evermore protruding belly. "Except for the birth of my daughter. That is the only plan I have at the moment."

As he returned his attention to Molly, he introduced his wife to Cat, then talk turned to Fortune Creek and how nothing ever happened there, followed by laughter. With that, the two of them said goodbye. Cat and Helen watched them leave, both looking after him with a little or a lot of awe. Cat felt relief to have him back since she'd been getting more uncomfortable with her pregnancy the past few days. Her daughter just seemed hell-bent to get out into the world.

THINGS IN THE Fortunate Creek Sheriff's Office soon returned to normal. Helen had moved on and was now knitting a huge throw in winter colors.

"It's a present for a friend," Helen said, as if Cat had asked. "Going to take me a while so I thought I'd start it now."

Cat realized she was going to miss the office, miss Fortune Creek. She'd told the sheriff the truth. She hadn't let herself think beyond the birth of her daughter. After that, she'd decide what she wanted to do, where she wanted them to live, what came next. Life had thrown her too many curveballs to make plans too far into the future. If she'd learned anything, it was that.

But Fortune Creek had warmed to her—and she to it. Ash had started coming across the street from the hotel a couple of times a week to bring her lunch courtesy of the local café. He'd bring a couple of lunch specials and they'd sit in her cramped office visiting.

Cat had looked forward to those visits to break up

her day. Ash told her about the ventriloquist who'd been murdered in his hotel before her time as sheriff. Since then he'd been trying to learn how to throw his voice, he told her. He'd practice at night, he said, but hadn't gotten it down yet.

It was strange, Cat thought. More people in town said hello to her and Helen was almost downright chatty on occasion. She realized that she felt more at home here in Fortune Creek. She'd been contacted with several job offers. But she was determined not to make any plans until after her daughter was born.

Cat spent the last few days as acting sheriff going through baby names online, trying to find the perfect one. She was thankful that the office gone back to being a place where nothing ever happened.

Until her water broke.

DYLAN COULDN'T WAIT to get back to the ranch—and Cat. They'd left things up in the air with him needing to go out to DC at the bequest of the prosecutor and Cat needing to tie up the loose ends of her case back in Fortune Creek.

He'd finally gotten the answers he'd desperately needed about his former boss, Allen Zimmerman.

"Turns out that his wife had been sick with cancer for several years," Ike told him. "I guess they didn't want anyone to know. But it drained them financially. Turns out also that Allen was deep in debt and about to lose his house just before his wife died. I guess he was desperate, and someone found out and took advantage."

Dylan wished his old boss had come to him. He would have gladly helped him out. But he suspected Allen had too much pride, so he'd sold out the men under him and his country. "Was it suicide?"

Ike nodded. "I think it was. He finally realized what he'd done. But not before he'd contacted your brother Beau."

Feeling a start, Dylan said, "Why would he do that?"

"It was originally thought that Beau was in on it, acting as an intermediary between the two countries. We now believe that he had tried to get Beau to get the list back."

"Why wouldn't he come to me?" Dylan demanded.

"Probably because you were married to Ginny Cooper," Ike said simply.

He swore and raked a hand through his hair. "So Beau—"

"Got hold of the thumb drive and left it for you to find because by then he must have known how deep this Russian cell was—or at least suspected as much. You were the only one he could trust."

"Is there any chance Ginny—"

Ike was already shaking his head before Dylan could finish.

"When she didn't get what she wanted, no doubt needed because of the people pulling her strings, she had Beau killed and faked her own death," Ike said.

Ike would never forgive Ginny for what she'd done. Ginny coming back from the dead had come as a shock to them both. Things had gotten ugly and dangerous at the end. He knew they were both lucky just to be alive. Ginny had admitted that she was driving the truck the night Cat's husband was killed. She and Luca had been hauling a load of stolen catalytic converters up to Canada that night. The sale would help finance more of their plans. It had been Ginny who'd left Taylor Jameson to die in his car beside the road.

Dylan was working on forgiving himself for marrying her, buying the place in Montana and leaving the keys in the old truck in the barn so she could drive it the night Taylor Jameson was killed.

Love was definitely blind since all he'd seen was surface beauty. If he had looked a little deeper…

He thought of Cat and how she radiated a warmth and compassion that made him want to be a better man. He ached for her in so many ways. She'd stolen a chunk of his heart from the very first. The more he was around her, the more he lost of his heart. He was totally taken with the woman, having never felt like this before. He couldn't imagine his life without her, and that scared him since he had no idea how she felt about him.

Now flying into Kalispell, it surprised him how much he'd missed the state. Montana had been a place to hide—but only temporarily. He'd never planned to stay there—not with that large house full of the hopes and dreams he'd had with Ginny, a reminder of everything bad that had happened. A part of him had always thought he'd go back to DC.

But that had changed when he met Cat. He realized he had no desire to be anywhere but on the ranch—with her. The big house was gone, thankfully burned to the ground with everything Ginny had put in it. He wondered why she'd bothered to decorate it. Had she hoped they would make a life there—after she finished her mission for her native country?

He thought again of the house, recalling how Ginny

had taken the old truck from the barn to make the run to Canada that had killed Cat's husband. She'd never planned to live there. Like everything else, the house had been a means to an end.

Grass would grow on the site and all memory of Ginny and the house would be gone forever, he told himself. He would have to rebuild. He'd thought about the house he would want if his dreams came true. That was up to Cat. He hated to get his hopes up since he knew he was getting ahead of himself even thinking about them living together with their babies and needing more room than the cottage could accommodate.

He still had to ask Cat to marry him. Hell, he hadn't even asked her out on a date. Also, he still had to get his nephew adopted and the two of them settled in. But he found himself looking forward to the future full of hope.

Dylan couldn't believe the twisted path his life with Ginny had taken and how it ended the way it had. He knew it wasn't his fault all the terrible things Ginny had done, but if he'd never met her... He would have never met Cat, he told himself. He was just thankful that out of all the bad, it had brought Cat and her baby into his life. Soon he would have his brother's son. He'd been thinking about names, since it was time Baby Doe had one. But he wanted to see what Cat thought.

Dylan couldn't wait to bring his brother's and Athena's child home to the ranch. He was so thankful that Beau's name had been cleared. Ginny had used him, threatening the lives of people he cared about to force him to help her. Beau being Beau had thought she was trying to get away from her birth land and the pressure on her from people who wanted to destroy the US.

But in fact, Ginny had been acting as a double agent the whole time, betraying both countries—and his brother.

He tried to push thoughts of the past away as the plane flew toward Kalispell, Montana. He had so many plans, all of them involving Cat. He just hoped she felt the same way about him.

The moment his plane landed, he turned his phone back on and saw that he had a text from a woman named Helen Graves.

Cat is in labor. She's gone to Kalispell to the hospital.

ONCE IN HIS PICKUP, Dylan drove straight to the hospital. He hated the thought of Cat having this baby alone even as he questioned if she would want him there. He hurried into the hospital, went to the desk and asked where the maternity ward was.

"Are you the father?" the nurse asked. He smiled, clearly anxious and trying to come up with an answer that would get him in to see Cat. The nurse took that as a yes. "Glad you made it. Come with me." She headed down the hall and he followed, wincing at the thought of what would happen when the nurse found out the truth. That truth could come quickly, he realized as they reached the room, and both stepped inside.

Cat lay on the bed, clearly in labor. She saw him, her eyes widening as she breathed through a contraction.

"Your husband made it in time," the nurse announced.

Cat looked from the nurse to Dylan. He gave a slight shrug and an embarrassed smile. She nodded and held out her hand and he stepped to her bedside and took it in his. She closed her eyes and breathed for a few moments as the contraction passed before another one started.

"I think we'd better have the doctor to take a look," the nurse said after checking her.

"What can I do?" Dylan asked. She squeezed his hand in answer, so he just held on to her as another contraction began.

A doctor came into the room and moved to the end of the bad. "Sounds like you're just about there," he said. "This is your husband?" Cat didn't answer as she focused on her breathing.

"Dylan," he said, introducing himself to the doctor. "What can I do to help?"

The doctor laughed. "Looks like you're doing it. Your first, huh? Get ready, you're about to become a father."

He swallowed the lump that had risen in his throat and looked at Cat. Tears burned his eyes, and he squeezed her hand.

Moments later nurses came in and things got hectic. Dylan kept his eyes on Cat, holding onto her, wishing there was more he could do.

Then he heard the baby suddenly begin to cry loudly. The doctor said, "Got yourself a healthy baby girl. Great set of lungs on her too," he added chuckling as the nurse cut the cord, took the baby for a few moments then handed her back wrapped in a blanket.

The baby in his arms, the doctor moved to the opposite side of the bed and laid the baby into her mother's arms. "Congratulations. You have a name for her yet?"

Cat shook her head, tears running down her face as she looked at her daughter. Dylan had to fight his own emotions, a lump so big in his throat that he couldn't speak if he had to. Then Cat looked over at him. "You want to hold her?"

She didn't wait for an answer as she handed over the tiny bundle. He couldn't believe how perfect she was. "She's beautiful," he breathed. "Just like her mama."

CAT WOKE TO find Dylan stretched out asleep on the cot next to her bed. She noted the stubble that darkened his jaw, his wrinkled shirt, his legs that were almost too long for the makeshift bed that had been brought in.

Between them was the bassinet with her beautiful daughter sleeping soundly. She wanted to wake her just to hold her, but didn't, thankful that they'd both gotten some rest. The past few weeks she'd had a terrible time getting comfortable at night. As much as she kept telling herself that she couldn't wait for the baby to be born, she kind of missed having her tucked protectively inside her body. She missed that closeness, feeling her growing, watching her own body changing as the time came.

Now she would have to watch from the sidelines.

"She's going to be just like you."

Cat looked up into Dylan's face. "I didn't know you were awake." He lay on his side staring at her—and her daughter. "Thank you for being here."

"Thank you for allowing me to. I wouldn't have missed it for the world. It was amazing." He held her gaze. "You were amazing. I was already in awe of you, but now…"

She felt her cheeks heat under his gaze. "Women give birth every day."

"You really aren't good at taking compliments," he said, smiling. "I have such respect for all those women, but especially for you." He glanced into the bassinet. "Have you thought about a name yet?"

"Not yet. How was DC?"

Dylan kept looking at her daughter. "I'll tell you all about it later. Your sheriff back?" She nodded. "I filed all the paperwork to get my nephew. Now it's just waiting and reading lots of books about babies and childrearing. I'm terrified."

Cat looked at her sleeping daughter. "Me too. I thought I was ready, but maybe there is never any way to get ready for your first child."

"Especially when you never expected it," he agreed.

"Especially. We both were surprised. At least I had nine months to prepare myself. You're going to do great."

He sat up and she could tell he was going to leave. "You're going to do great too. I heard you're busting out of here. If you need a ride, a place to stay…"

"The sheriff has insisted I remain in the apartment over the office for at least a month before I make any big decisions. He and his wife are building on his ranch outside of town and living at the hotel until the house is finished."

"You think you'll stay in law enforcement?"

"Not sure about law enforcement. I just want to spend time with my daughter for a while before I decide."

Dylan nodded and slipped off the bed to stand. "If you need anything, call me. But I'll be keeping in touch. What about a ride tomorrow?"

"Ash from the hotel insisted on picking us up but thank you. And Dylan, thank you again for being here. Let me know how it goes with your nephew."

"Don't worry, I will. See you soon."

She could tell that there was more he wanted to say. She felt the same way, but right now, it felt too soon, so she let him walk away.

Chapter Twenty-Two

"You have visitors," the nurse said from the hospital room doorway a few hours later.

Helen came through the door first, followed by the sheriff and his wife, Molly, then residents of Fortune Creek, including Ash. They came with flowers, chocolate and cute baby clothes.

But what touched Cat the most was the present from Helen, a knitted pink sweater and booties. She looked up, tears in her eyes. "These are so adorable. Helen, thank you."

The older woman looked embarrassed. "She's going to need something to wear until it warms up. This is also for you." She handed over a large wrapped bundle. It was the blanket she'd been working on those past few weeks before Cat had gone into labor.

Cat held it to her. "It's so soft and warm. Thank you so much."

Helen bobbed her head and said she needed to get back to the office. "Someone should be working," she said in the direction of the sheriff as she left.

Brandt chuckled. "Seems you and Helen got on just fine," he said, sounding surprised.

All Cat could do was smile. "I might have her teach me how to knit."

The sheriff's wife spoke up. "You're braver than me. I get the feeling she thinks I stole Brandt from her." They all laughed, especially Cat since she knew it was true.

Ash brought her the donuts she loved, then sat and visited for a while. Cat thought he really needed to find himself a good woman and told him so.

"Not every woman wants to come live in Fortune Creek in an old haunted hotel."

"Is it really haunted?" Cat asked in surprise.

"That's what they tell me," was all he would say.

Ash gave her and her daughter a ride back to her apartment over the sheriff's office the next day. Cat heard from Dylan. He'd gone to the state capital in Helena to finish the paperwork to get his nephew and buy more baby books.

"It's going to be fine," she told him, chuckling at how nervous he sounded. She'd seen what the man could do under pressure. She had no doubt that he could handle a baby. She'd also felt his love and affection and knew that his nephew was in great hands.

When she arrived at the apartment, there was a beautiful bassinet full of baby things and flowers, all from Dylan with a note that read, *According to the books I've been reading, these are things you're really going to need. D*

Cat smiled and found that he was right. She'd planned to let her daughter sleep with her for a while, unsure how long they would be in the upstairs apartment. Now that they were staying for a while, the bassinet was perfect.

She texted him a thank you.

You were right! I needed all of this! I just hadn't realized it yet. Thank you for such a thoughtful gift.

Time passed quickly as she found herself immersed in all things baby. In the meantime, she really needed to give her daughter a name. She had wanted to wait until the baby was born. Now that her darling little girl was here, she couldn't put it off any longer. The hospital had called again today about the birth certificate.

She finally decided on Lizzie Taylor Jameson, naming him after her mother, Elizabeth, and her daughter's father, Taylor.

Dylan called every evening, filling her in how things were going at the ranch. The ashes and debris from the big house had been carted away. A foundation would soon be laid for the new house.

For hours, they designed this new house, discussing what it should look like, what rooms were needed, what appliances it should have. For Cat it was like building a house online, just a dream of what she'd want if she ever got to design her own house. It was a game to her. She had no idea if Dylan even took her suggestions seriously.

They also talked about the adoption and how it was going. He'd gotten to spend time with his nephew so they also talked babies. He'd been reading baby books. When he learned about something that worked well, he would send the item to her as well as buy one for himself. Her apartment was now filled.

"Do babies really need all this?" she'd asked him, laughing.

"Apparently," he'd said. "Who knew?"

She often fell asleep talking to Dylan about everything from air fryers to unidentified aircraft he'd once seen. She knew his favorite color and he knew hers. He knew what kind of sheets she liked and why. Just as she knew what kind of coffee he preferred and how he was allergic to shellfish.

Often they would be giving a bottle to the babies when he called during his visitations with his nephew. Cat loved the closeness she shared with him.

In the meantime, she marveled at how Fortune Creek felt like home even though she'd been there for such a short time. It had been bumpy at first, trying to fill Sheriff Parker's big boots. But ultimately, she'd held her own.

With spring turning to early summer, she often took her daughter out in her expensive stroller—thank you, Dylan—for a walk around town. Everyone would make a point of coming out to greet them, so she got to know more residents. Sometimes she and her daughter would go to the café for lunch. Her daughter loved all the attention she got.

As she sat on the couch, she looked into the bassinet at Lizzie. It really had been such a thoughtful gift from Dylan, and she hoped she got to tell him so in person soon.

Her cell phone rang and she picked up at once when she saw it was Dylan.

"I'm downstairs. Is this a bad time?" he asked.

"It's a perfect time," she said. "Come on up. It doesn't lock anymore after Ginny let herself in." A few moments later, she opened the apartment door to him.

He handed her a bouquet of daisies. In his other hand was a baby carrier, and she realized she was finally going to meet the baby she'd been so anxious to see.

"The adoption went through!" she cried as she knelt down to pull back the small blanket to see his face.

"Oh, Dylan, he's beautiful. Come in, come in."

She took the flowers and put them in a vase while Dylan freed his nephew from the carrier. "Want to hold him?"

She nodded vigorously, and he placed the baby in her arms. "Oh, look at those bright blue eyes!"

"He and your daughter could be brother and sister," Dylan said as he came to stand next to her, both admiring the little boy. "He's grown so much since the first time I saw him."

Her daughter let out a squawk from her bassinet and they moved over to her.

"Thank you again for this," Cat said of the bassinet. She handed him the baby and picked up her own. "It's perfect."

"Just like your daughter. What did you end up naming her?"

She told him with a laugh. They had both agonized over naming the babies.

"I wanted to run it by you, but I had to give him a name for the adoption papers. Meet Beauregard James Walker, named after his father and, Beau's and my father."

"That is a mouthful," she said with a chuckle.

"That's why his nickname is BJ."

"I like that," she said and presented her daughter. "Meet Lizzie Taylor Jameson. Named after my mother Elizabeth and—"

"And your daughter's father," Dylan said. "I think it's wonderful. She looks like a Lizzie. She looks like you."

They stood awkwardly for a few moments. All the

hours they'd spent on the phone, they'd grown closer. But now being together after hardly seeing each other in person, they both felt shy.

"Any chance you're free for dinner?" he asked. "BJ and I are celebrating his six-month birthday out at the ranch tonight. I know it's late notice. I just realized the date."

"I'm having steak and salad. He'll be having formula, but it won't be long before he gets solids. Check out his two teeth," Dylan said like the proud father he was. "He is definitely a good eater. We'd love for the two of you to come."

Cat smiled. "We'd be delighted. Lizzie will be bringing her own bottle, but I'd love steak and salad. What can I bring?"

"Just you and Lizzie." Dylan's gaze met hers and held it. "Look at the two of us," he said smiling.

Epilogue

Cat moved to the porch at the sound of laughter. She couldn't help but smile at what she saw even as her heart raced a little. "Are you sure about this?" she asked her husband a little anxiously.

Dylan laughed and turned to the two children sitting astride the horse next to him. BJ had his arms around his sister who had one hand resting on the saddle horn. Both gave her a toothy grin. Both were dressed in what they called their cowboy outfits. Checked shirts, jeans and cowboy boots and hats.

"I rode my first horse at two," Dylan said.

"We're almost three!" the two children said almost in unison. Since they'd become brother and sister, they often finished each other's sentences. Anyone who didn't know their separate stories would have sworn they were hers and Dylan's biological children. BJ and Lizzie were inseparable, both growing like weeds, both unaware of how they had come into the world. Cat knew they wouldn't be able to protect them from finding out some-day, but for now they were just the intricate part of this family she and Dylan had made.

Cat often looked back, wondering how things had

turned out like they had. Dylan had invited her and Lizzie to dinner at the ranch. There were other dates after that, both of them bringing their babies. She often wondered what people thought—not that she cared. She was too happy being with Dylan and BJ. Lizzie and BJ had taken to each other from the start. Instantly babbling together, later crawling after each other and now trying to outdo each other.

On Beau's six-month birthday and the first time he got solids, Dylan asked her to marry him. She remembered his face in the flickering light of his son's single birthday candle, him on his knees putting a beautiful diamond on her finger. She'd said yes.

Their wedding was held at the ranch. Dylan invited a few people from his past, but not many. Same with Cat. All of Fortune Creek had turned out. A barbecue had followed with local beef and pork on a spit. The day ended with them putting their children to bed. It had been perfect.

Since then, life had only gotten better, she realized as her hand went to her protruding belly and the two babies snuggled in there. Another boy and girl. She thought of the way Dylan had been shocked when they'd gotten the news.

"But I'm sterile," he said to the doctor.

"Apparently not," the doctor had said with a laugh. "Why don't we run some tests." They had. Cat was surprised Dylan had taken the news so well. There was a reason Ginny had been taking birth control pills. Dylan wasn't sterile. His results had been doctored to make him think he couldn't have children.

"How did we get so lucky?" he asked as if in awe.

Had it been luck? Or fate? She liked to think it had been love. There was no denying the immediate attraction she'd felt for Dylan. He'd apparently felt the same way. After going through everything they had, the danger had drawn them even closer together.

They seldom talked about the events that had brought them here or what they'd had to go through before becoming a family. Cat had realized that she wasn't going back into law enforcement. She had babies to raise with her husband.

They often joked about what they would tell the kids when asked how their parents met.

"How about this," Dylan had suggested one night as they lay in their king bed in their newly finished house. "Mommy came out to the ranch to arrest me."

Cat had laughed and said, "Daddy saved me from his evil houseguest with a crush on him."

"Not even funny," he'd said as he rolled her over on top of him and kissed her. There had been an agreement between them when it came to having children. "How about we have as many as we can afford," he'd suggested.

"Not a chance," Cat had said, shocked when she'd found out how much her husband was worth. "Let's just see how it goes."

They'd created the twins she now carried that night. Four children had a nice ring to it, but if she knew her husband—and she did—there would be more. BJ and Lizzie were already excited to meet their new siblings. Cat often marveled that Beau's start in life hadn't seemed to affect the sweet, thoughtful and caring child. Dylan said his namesake had been the same way. Cat knew that was probably what had gotten her husband's brother into trouble. Lizzie was a spitfire like her mother.

"You wanted her to be just like me," she reminded Dylan often. He would always laugh and nod and say, "Right, be careful what you wish for."

It had been a grand day when they'd moved into their new home that she and Dylan had designed with children in mind. It was a warm and welcoming place that often saw visitors from Fortune Creek. The sheriff and Dylan had hit it off, talking horses and ranching.

Brandt and Molly had finished their house just in time since Molly was pregnant. The four of them had become close, often having dinner at each other's houses. Both were great with BJ and Lizzie, though Cat often saw fear in their eyes at the thought of having one of their own.

When Molly announced that she was having a girl, Cat had reassured her the child would be nothing like Lizzie with her bright red hair, mass of freckles and stubborn, fiery disposition, all of which seemed to make Dylan love the child even more. Cat felt as if BJ was hers, the baby she'd almost delivered in her office, the Baby Doe who'd gone missing that she'd prayed would be found, the baby that she'd held in her arms even before Dylan had gotten to hold him. BJ was hers, just as Lizzie was Dylan's. He'd been there when she was born. He'd bought her first bassinet. He'd saved her mother's life.

Helen often drove out to the ranch, offering babysitting services. They had finally taken her up on it one Saturday and had gone into Kalispell for dinner. When they returned they hadn't known what to expect.

They found both children were tucked in bed sound asleep and Helen knitting next to the fireplace.

"Any trouble?" Cat asked suspiciously.

"None at all," Helen said.

"Not even from Lizzie?" she'd asked disbelieving. "We've been having a time getting her to stay in her bed at night."

Helen shook her head. "It might be the way you tell her to go to bed."

Cat was afraid to ask.

The older woman smiled. "Maybe it's the tone of my voice, but children seem to listen to me when I speak."

She'd laughed as she'd looked over at Dylan who was grinning. "Thank you so much." But when she offered Helen money, she'd declined.

"It was my pleasure. I enjoyed them. They're very bright children. Like their parents." With that she rose to leave.

"Stay the night," Dylan said, but Helen declined again.

"I know that road like the back of my hand. I'll be fine. I actually enjoy the trip out here."

"Then you'll be back Sunday for dinner," Cat said and Helen smiled.

"I'd like that."

"Ash is coming out with a date," she told her former coworker.

Helen wrinkled her nose. "What a woman from eastern Montana was doing over here is anyone's guess."

Cat knew how Helen felt about outsiders—even ones from the same state. "I've heard she is delightful." Helen huffed at that as she gathered up her things to leave.

"Helen, thank you again," Dylan said and only got a grunt as he walked her to her car, Cat watching them.

"How did you win that woman over?" he asked as he joined her on the porch to watch Helen drive away.

"I have no idea," she said with a laugh and turned to her husband. "How did I win you over?"

"It was that silver star on your tan uniform," he said pulling her into a hug. "How could I not have fallen for you? A woman with more freckles than stars in the sky and eyes bluer than Montana skies."

She chuckled as they stood like that looking out at all the stars over the mountains, both content in a way she doubted either of them had ever known before.

Looking up at the night sky, Cat wondered what Taylor and Beau would have thought of this family she and Dylan had formed. She found herself smiling as the stars twinkled above them, and she nestled deeper into her husband's arms. She felt sure they would have been happy to see how things had ended.

* * * * *